MY BIG FAT FAKE MATRIMONIAL AD

A BEAVER RUN FAKE RELATIONSHIP ROMANCE

BRIE WILDS

RUTTISH
PRESS

Published by Ruttish Press, Sparta

eISBN: 978-1-63589-746-3
ISBN: 978-1-63589-760-9

Editor: Kasi Alexander
Cover Design: Brie Wilds

GET MY NEWSLETTER
Want to receive the latest information on my upcoming novels and receive a
FREE book? Sign up for my newsletter by clicking on Brie Wilds
Newsletter or visit www.briewilds.com

PRAISE FOR BRIE WILDS

…this is the first book that I have read by this author, but it will definitely not be my last. The storyline had me from the get-go!!! Character interaction, plot, everything was fantastic!!! Wow! I have to say, this story checked all the boxes for me!!! So if you're looking for a fun and sexy read, look no further!

Happy reading everyone!.

— MELINDA S

The characters interact beautifully and the story line intriguing.

— AIMEE L

PROLOGUE

MASON

MASON SUTTON COULDN'T BELIEVE HE WAS SITTING ON A plane. He was supposed to be at Cupid Cabana on Valentine's day. If he missed his flight or got delayed, he might not make it to the restaurant on the magical day. A lot was at stake.

He needed to find a girl and get engaged before the end of February. And married twelve months from the engagement or lose a fortune. His grandfather, to keep the family name going, had stipulated that condition in his Will, and today was February the 13th.

He'd had a series of bad luck at dating. His ex-fiancée, a computer engineer, had blatantly cheated on him, and they'd parted ways. Mason wanted someone he could trust. His luck had not held.

It was a dealbreaker meeting someone and telling them you wanted to get engaged right away. If he told them the reason, maybe they'd agree. But then that would put him back in the same situation as his ex—no love. Just waiting for a payday.

His mind drifted back to that phone conversation with his buddy Sam Stone when he'd come up with an insane suggestion. Visit Cupid Cabana on Valentine's Day and make a wish while caressing Cupid's arrow on a statue of the mythical god.

"What?" asked Mason, not sure he'd heard right.

"Cupid grants every wish on Valentine's Day. It's like touching the statue of John Harvard at the Harvard Yard," Stone had said. "You remember Harvard?"

"That's an old wives' tale."

"But you did caress his shoes," said Stone, "and you did get laid. What's her name again? The one in our freshman year at MIT…Nancy!"

At the other end of the phone call, Mason nodded, remembering that drunken night many years ago. They had been escorting their dates to their room and saw the statue in the yard. He'd rubbed his hand on John Harvard's bronze shoe, made a wish, and a frigid Nancy was all over him when they got back to her room. Then he thought it was the alcohol, but now Stone begged to differ.

"Same concept," said Stone. "But here, you're dealing with the god of erotic love, attraction, and desire. Touch Cupid's arrowhead on the restaurant's statue, and the god will shine on you. He'll shoot an arrow on your behalf straight into the heart of the woman"—there was a pause—"or man you desire. Just kidding!"

Mason, on speakerphone, crossed his hands over his chest and rolled his eyes. Moreover, the mythological god looked like a toddler. Shouldn't a grownup god be taking care of adult matters like allure and erotic love? It sounded like an assertion you swallowed with a bag of salt.

Stone continued, "It's like religion—"

It was like Stone read his mind, thought Mason.

"It needs a heavy dose of faith. And remember, desperate times require desperate measures."

Just then, the pilot's voice came over the loudspeaker, bringing Mason back to the present.

"CABIN CREW, PREPARE FOR TAKEOFF."

ON HIS LAP WAS A DUNKIN DONUTS BAG WITH HIS breakfast, a toasted croissant stuffed with bacon, sausage, egg, and cheese. The delicious smell wafted up to his nose, but the food was the furthest thing from his mind. Mason had a death grip on his seat's armrest, his stomach tied in knots. No room for even a morsel of that mouthwatering meal.

His stomach was so wound tight he could have been constipated, sitting on the porcelain throne executing a Valsalva maneuver.

Mason hated flying and would have gladly driven the thirteen hours to the small town outside Atlanta, Georgia, if not for his date with Cupid. He'd never taken a job that would have him physically travel this far before. Most jobs he took were online, even if the clients were on the West Coast.

He ran his plan through his mind. It was straightforward and simple. Fly in, extract the girl, and fly out. That would be a lot of flying in twenty-four hours. But that was the only way to get the job done and still get back to Jersey in time for Valentine's Day and his rendezvous with Cupid.

He could have said no to this assignment, but it was more like a follow-up to the last September job. And he didn't want to let down his good friend Sam Stone, who'd recommended him for the job.

He and Sam went back a long way, starting at Phillips Academy in Andover, Massachusetts. Then MIT, where they both got degrees in computer science and engineering. Either of them could have ended up in Silicon Valley, but again they shared an affinity for law enforcement. Mason liked being an investigator, where his computer skills would be put to good use.

Dr. Sanjay Patel had called him a few hours ago. His twenty-five-year-old daughter had taken off again, he'd said. There was just a trace of an accent in his voice. But this time, she seemed to be in trouble, he explained. When Mason inquired what the concern was, he told him it seemed she had been robbed in a small town close to Atlanta. Her phone and money were stolen.

She didn't want to involve the police, and now she was too scared to venture out of the hotel. Mason's assignment was to go to Georgia and bring her back to Beaver Run.

The jet's engines roared in his ear as the pilot revved up for the final sprint down the runway for wheels up. Mason tensed up, turning his athletic six-foot-two-inch frame into one rigid mass as the plane raced down the runway. He felt like his heart was forced into his stomach as the plane lifted off.

Once the jet leveled off in the sky, Mason's breathing came back to normal, and his muscles relaxed, but his mind was restless.

After what seemed like an eternity, the pilot's voice came over the loudspeaker.

"CABIN CREW, PREPARE FOR LANDING."

. . .

THE PLANE DROPPED ALTITUDE AT INTERVALS TRIGGERING A repeat of all the emotions he'd felt during takeoff.

Then the plane touched down smoothly on the tarmac. The pilot hit the brakes and threw the engines into reverse to slow the aircraft. Mason let out a sigh of relief. They were safely on the ground. They'd made it.

Suddenly he heard and felt a rumble, and the plane made a sharp right turn.

Shrieks of terror rose in the cabin as the plane skidded onto the grass.

Overhead cabins clicked open. Carry-ons flew out like bats rushing out of a cave in every direction.

The plane came to an abrupt stop.

Mason lunged forward, hitting his head on the chair in front of him.

1

PRIYANKA DESCENDED THE SMALL FLIGHT OF STAIRS INTO THE lobby. Last night she'd used the elevator, not knowing the short flight of stairs in the middle of her floor led straight to the reception area.

Dressed in a white blouse, a gray skirt, a jeans jacket, and with her black shoulder-length hair down, she walked into the lobby. Her eyes darted all over the place, trying to make out who her father had sent to escort her back. Nobody caught her attention as not belonging. Everybody seemed to be headed in one direction as if following an invisible line. She followed it too—the smell of coffee.

She'd barely slept a wink and needed some caffeine in her system to remain awake. After her ordeal last night, she was surprised she wasn't still freaking out and remained holed up in her hotel room. Maybe the fact that help was on the way bolstered her.

Priyanka still couldn't believe how easy it was for her

7

phone and handbag to be stolen in a busy area. Thank God she was too immobilized by fear and surprise to react. They could have assaulted her. People's first instinct when their property is stolen right in front of them is to try to retrieve it, and that's when they get hurt. Most of the time, the thief has a plan B, which is usually violence.

A section of the lobby had been transformed into a breakfast area. Priyanka's stomach growled and rumbled with delight at the spread and smells. Her borborygmi were drowned out by the sounds of conversations and cutlery, just like her mother had drowned out her protests at home about meeting potential marriage candidates.

She stood behind a woman and waited her turn to get a plate and a bowl. She watched the other hotel guests helping themselves to eggs, sausages, waffles, toast, bagels, cakes, pancakes—you name it. She placed her bowl on the plate, got some mixed fruits and yogurt, and then poured herself a cup of coffee, adding cream and sugar.

She'd planned to take her food back to her room but needed to stay in the open. Her gaze drifted around the lobby, looking for an empty table.

A man got up from a table a few feet from her and walked away, leaving his dirty plate behind. She thought nothing of it until he headed toward the bank of elevators. Priyanka watched him get on. She shrugged and walked over to the table. She put down her plate, grabbed his with a napkin, walked over to the garbage, and dumped it.

The wall clock by the receptionist showed it was just after nine in the morning. Her father had assured her the man would be on the first flight out. He'd given her a name, but no description. She'd heard something like Jason Mutton.

Priyanka sipped her coffee and felt her body relax. Her thoughts drifted to last night when she'd taken a walk to clear her head and get some air. She'd sat on a bench in a nearby park when three men walked by talking. They stopped and asked her for directions while one sat beside her. After she told them she was new in the area and had no idea, the tallest of them, about six feet or more, asked to borrow her phone.

"Sure," said Priyanka even as an uneasy feeling crept into her stomach.

He punched in some numbers, started talking, and casually walked away as if seeking privacy. The one sitting next to her got up, joined the second guy, and they walked away.

It crossed her mind they were stealing from her. But it couldn't be. People were there. Then she reached for her handbag, but it was gone.

Her heart pounding, Priyanka jumped to her feet. "Hey!"

One of the men turned around and faced her. He placed a finger to his lips and walked backward.

Her heart pounded in her chest like galloping horses. Heat rushed through her body. She wanted to run after them and retrieve her property. But with three against one, she had no chance.

Thank goodness her father's words rushed into her head at that moment. Material things could be replaced, but life, once it's cut short, is gone. She got up from the bench and headed back to the hotel as fast as she could.

The irony of what happened was not lost on her. She'd meant to send a message to her parents by vanishing for a few days to a small town she'd randomly picked on the map. Instead, she was the one being sent a message. Rash decisions could be dangerous.

The clatter of plates and cutlery as a hotel staff cleared a nearby table brought her back from her reminiscing.

She finished her food and, still not seeing anybody, went to the reception counter. A woman in a black suit, skirt suit, and white shirt attended to her. "Hello, I'm staying in room 106. Do I have any messages?"

"Hi." She flashed Priyanka a big smile. "Just one second, let me check." She looked through some sheets on a clipboard and shook her head. "Nope."

"Okay, thank you." Priyanka smiled and went back to her room.

She debated placing another call from her room to her father, then changed her mind. She would wait a little longer. She felt naked without her phone.

Priyanka put a *do not disturb* sign on the door to keep housekeeping at bay. She stretched out on her bed and glanced at the bedside clock; it was 9:40 a.m. She would go back to the lobby in twenty minutes after a short nap.

Priyanka didn't know how long she'd slept, but the sound of a ringing phone felt like something poking at her ear. She opened her eyes, and the ringing stopped. She looked at the time—it was 12.15 p.m. "Oh shit."

She sprang to her feet, went to the bathroom, peed, splashed water on her face, and came back to the room. Relief washed over her. It must have been the front desk calling. At last, help had arrived. She sat on the bed and put on her ankle boots. Her bag was packed and ready.

Priyanka literally flew down the stairs to the lobby, confident she would be in Beaver Run in the next few hours. She scanned the lobby as she walked down the stairs, looking for anyone out of place. A couple exited the hotel through the automatic doors—not them.

A man walked briskly to the elevator, pushed a button, and waited. Maybe. Then she locked eyes with a gorgeous looking guy sitting on one of the lobby couches. Square jaw, black hair with an eye color she couldn't really describe.

10

Well, well, who is that? Move along, Pri, nothing to see there.
She pulled her eyes away from him.

At the counter, the same lady she'd spoken to earlier smiled, raised a finger, and walked away. Priyanka nodded. She knew the sign—*I'll be with you in one second.* A few moments later, the receptionist hadn't returned. Tapping her finger on the counter, she pretended to look around again as she stole one more glance at the hunk. Wow, he was looking at her. She glanced away.

Now, if she weren't going home today, maybe she'd found a guy to tumble. Have fast unattached sex with a stranger and let out some tension. The thought tickled her. She'd always walked the straight and narrow path. She'd defied her mother when she went away to college and found herself a boyfriend.

He'd taken her virginity, and after he graduated, left for India to run their family business. When they were dating, she'd thought he was the one. Maybe her mother was right after all. Arranged marriages and not love was the way to go.

She still needed time to finish her paintings without her mother showing up in her studio in the attic with one matrimonial ad or the other for her to check out.

But a one-night stand—her heart wouldn't be involved, and it would be quick. Her parents wouldn't know.

It would be just sex, full of her fantasies. Priyanka's girly parts twitched. She pulled at the collar of her blouse, feeling suddenly hot.

She glanced at the subject of her desire, and to her surprise, he was still looking at her. She about-faced, looking for the receptionist. From the corner of her eyes, she noticed the man was now standing.

Priyanka turned. His physique looked familiar, like one of the guys that had taken her phone last night. She pushed off the counter and took long strides to the stairs. Once in front of her door, hands shaking, she inserted the key card. She pushed open the door as soon as it flashed green. She entered and put on the door safety chain.

Her pulse raced. Was it the guy from last night? It had been dark, but... She leaned against the door. Why did she panic and run? He was just another tall guy.

She heard a sound and stopped breathing. Someone was knocking on her door. She looked through the peephole and couldn't make out who was there—too close. Was it one of the guys that had stolen her phone last night? They intercepted her calls.

"Ms. Patel? I know you're there," said a deep, confident-sounding male voice.

Priyanka froze.

"My name is Mason Sutton. Your father sent me to bring you back."

What was she going to do?

"Let me call him so you can speak to him."

She heard dialing on the speaker, and the phone started to ring. Her father's voice came on, and she pulled the door open with the safety chain on. It was the hunk from the lobby, all right.

"THIS IS DR. PATEL. I CAN'T COME TO THE PHONE RIGHT NOW. Leave your name, number, and a brief message, and I'll get back to you. At the tone, please leave a message. Beep."

"VOICE MAIL," SAID THE GUY. "I JUST SPOKE TO HIM." HE tapped his screen. The phone rang and went to voice mail again. The man shook his head and raised his head. "Sorry

I'm late. I had a rough morning. Are you ready?" He eyed the chain. "Okay. Do you want to meet me at the lobby?"

She thought for a moment. "Okay, I'll meet you downstairs."

"Sounds good."

Priyanka slammed the door shut. What if it was a ploy to grab her? He could easily overpower her. That iPhone could be hers, taken out of the case. What if he was working with the guys from last night? They could have hacked into her phone and worked out a plan to kidnap her. She had to get away.

She grabbed her bag and walked over to the sliding door for the balcony. She stepped onto the balcony and shut the door behind her. The hotel had different levels, and the first floor was just a few feet from the ground. The wall was some type of fancy block with flowered vines attached to it. Priyanka didn't hesitate. She tossed her bag over and started down.

As she climbed, looking down to her left for a place to place her foot, she felt a breeze in places that didn't get that air when she was clothed.

Priyanka looked to her right. Her skirt had hooked onto the vine somehow, and as she climbed down, it had pulled up to her waist. Her butt was exposed to anyone watching.

She quickly unhooked her skirt and decided to drop down since she was close to the ground. She landed on her tiptoes.

Pulse racing and still flushed from the embarrassment, she patted her clothes down and bent to pick her bag. When she straightened up, she almost jumped out of her skin.

Mason Sutton stood there grinning and fanning himself. "What a view. What happened? The elevator wasn't working?"

2

MASON

MASON'S PANTS GOT TIGHT RIGHT AWAY. HE TURNED AWAY, giving the gorgeous woman a few minutes to regain her composure.

He ran through his mind how he'd come to see the sexiest, rounded ass he'd ever set eyes on. His mind drifted back to the plane.

The events after the plane had skidded off were still sketchy in his mind. He remembered hitting his head on the seat in front of him. It was just a little bump.

The nose of the plane was down when it came to rest. Soon the doors opened, the crew activated the escape chutes, and evacuation started.

Apart from scrapes and cuts, miraculously, no one had any serious injuries. They were driven by bus to a makeshift rescue center inside the airport. Medical personnel examined them, then the airline or airport staff asked a few questions about what happened.

Then they were free to leave. Passengers that needed or wanted more help like counseling or travel changes stayed on. That wasn't him. Mason had had no luggage, so he'd found his way to the car rental desk, rented a Nissan Pathfinder, and was on his way to meet Priyanka. The whole debriefing took over three hours.

The car smelled of cigarettes even though Mason had requested a non-smoker car. Maybe all his senses were still in a heightened state. Adrenaline still sloshing around inside him from the high of the crash landing.

He turned on the car's wiper to get rid of rain on the windshield. Maybe the runway had been slippery from the rain.

Mason felt good about himself. The dread and bitter taste of fear that had coated his tongue was now gone. He felt confident as he eased into traffic and followed his phone's GPS directions.

Finding the hotel hadn't been difficult, but getting a hold of Priyanka Patel had been.

The hotel was one of those gems from another era tucked away in the suburbs, off the beaten path. They got overflow traffic from bigger cities around, but they became your favorite place once you discovered them. It had a home away from home feeling to it.

He got there just before noon. The sun was up, and the rain clouds were gone.

Dressed in jeans, a white button-down shirt, and a V-neck sweater, Mason was comfortable. He tossed his lightweight jacket back in the car and walked into the hotel.

Mason looked around the lobby with a combination of fabric and leather couches, tables with tall stools arranged in different sections creating a living room like setting. He'd expected to see a young girl pacing about, but he didn't. A couple sat on one of the couches, their eyes glued to the TV.

The receptionist flashed Mason a big smile, and he walked over to her, returning the smile. "Hi."

"Hello. Welcome. How can I help you?"

"I'm looking for a guest here…"

"Do you have a name?"

"Yes. Priyanka Patel. She's expecting me."

"Oh."

Mason saw the flash of disappointment on the receptionist's face. But she recognized the name.

She lowered her head and looked at a sheet attached to a clipboard.

"Yes, I'll call her room and let her know you're here. And you're…?"

"Mason, Mason Sutton."

She held the phone to her ear and, after a few moments, shook her head. "She's not answering. She was down here a few hours ago. Let's give it a few minutes, and I'll call back." She pointed toward the sitting arrangement. "Why don't you make yourself comfortable, and I'll let you know once she answers. You can help yourself to coffee or tea over there."

"Thank you. I appreciate it." Mason dialed Dr. Patel as soon as she sat down. He told him about the delay at the airport and that he was at the hotel.

"That's terrible. I'm glad you're okay. Listen, I'm at the hospital. Call me once you're with Pri, and thank you so much."

"No problem." The line went dead. Mason looked up toward the receptionist's counter, and his heart literally stopped. Looking at him was the most beautiful girl he'd ever seen. Jet black hair, round eyes, and full lips he wouldn't mind feasting on. She had long, shapely killer legs. He would consider it illegal to cover them with pants or jeans. They were designed for shorts, skirts, and ankle-length boots. And she was checking him out.

He hadn't seen Cupid yet, but the Greek god was already at work. What would happen if he touched his arrowhead? Women would be tossing their panties at him. Then the girl turned and bolted.

He pulled up the picture Dr. Patel had sent on his phone. That was Priyanka. He went after her, but she made it to her room fast. For some reason, she was reluctant to let him into her room. Then he couldn't get hold of her father on the phone to reassure her. He didn't blame her, considering she had been attacked last night.

They agreed to meet downstairs. He was by the elevator when his sixth sense kicked in. This bird was going to fly. He saw the sign that said stairs and headed for it. He took them two at a time and went outside. He'd just made it to a quiet corner of the building where he figured Priyanka's room was when he saw her round ass in a black thong hanging in the air.

"My God," said Mason, his voice barely audible. His jeans felt tight. He would give anything to sink his cock into that pussy.

Priyanka dropped to the ground, then bent to pick up her bag. "What the?" She jerked back once she saw Mason.

Mason grinned. "What a view. What happened? The elevator wasn't working?"

"Hello? Are you just going to stand there with a grin on your face?"

Her voice brought Mason back to the present. "Sorry, I was just processing what I saw. I apologize in advance, but you have a great ass."

Her nostrils flared. "You didn't just say that," she said through clenched teeth.

Mason went on the offensive. He had enough drama for a lifetime. "Were you running from me? Don't you want to go home? Hold on, let's call your daddy again." Mason raised his phone and tapped the screen. He put the phone on speaker.

"Sorry, I mistook you for one of the men that attacked me last night."

"Moi?" said Mason in an exaggerated French accent. "I just made it by the skin of my teeth this morning. The plane skidded on—"

"Hello! Mr. Sutton? Do you have her?" Dr. Patel's voice came over the speaker.

"Daddy!"

"Pri! My little princess. Thank God you're safe. Oh, your mother will be delighted. She's sick with worry."

"Yeah right," said Priyanka.

Hmmm, thought Mason.

"She meant well, Pri, don't blame her. I'm at the hospital…I have to go. Mr. Sutton will—"

"Call me Mason, sir," said Mason.

Dr. Patel laughed. "Okay, Mason, I'm Sanjay. Pri, Mason will take care of you. I'll call once I'm done with surgery, okay? Bye."

Mason put his phone away. "Now we've cleared up my identity, let's start over." He raised his hand for a handshake. "I'm Mason, and your father has instructed me to bring you back to New Jersey. And you're Pri."

"No, Priyanka to you. Only my family and close friends call me Pri."

"Okay. I'm Mason. My family and friends call me… Mason." He exhaled noisily. "We have to check you out officially in case someone saw you climbing down and jumped to a different conclusion."

She shot him a look.

"You…you know, settle any outstanding bills. We don't want the police coming after us."

Priyanka nodded.

Back inside the hotel, Mason gave the receptionist his business credit card to replace Priyanka's since her dad had canceled hers. Ten minutes later, they were on the highway.

Mason had a lot of questions, but they could wait. There would be more than enough time for chatting. "Do you need anything to eat, drink? We can stop at a gas station."

"No, I'm fine."

They drove for another ten minutes before Priyanka turned sharply to face him. "You just passed the exit for ATL airport."

"I know. We're driving."

Priyanka's eyes widened. "What? All the way to New Jersey? That's like twelve and a half hours."

He touched his phone on the air vent magnetic mount. "The GPS says thirteen hours plus."

She let out a strangled laugh and swiped her hair behind her left ear. Words sputtered out of her mouth as she struggled to find what to say. "But I thought you flew in? What now? You're suddenly scared of flying?"

"Haha, very funny. But yes, I'm petrified of flying."

"So all this macho physique is all for show?"

Mason yanked his phone out of the air vent and gave it to her. "Here. Google news, Atlanta airport."

Reluctantly she took the phone and started typing. "What am I going to see? They closed the airspace for a game of *Quidditch*?"

"Huh? Qui what?"

There was silence as she read. Then her head shot up. "A plane crash-landed this morning. Where you on…?"

"If you'd listened when I came to the hotel, that's why I was late. Normally I'm scared of flying. But after that plane skidded off the runway after touching down safely, I'm driving everywhere until further notice."

Priyanka drew in a deep breath and exhaled. She sat back on her seat and placed her right foot on the dashboard. Her skirt rode up, exposing succulent thighs.

Mason started having a hard time maintaining the Pathfinder in a straight line. He decided to satisfy his curiosity. He turned to her. "Can I have my phone back? I need it for directions."

In his periphery, he saw her hold up the phone, but it didn't register. After a moment, she said, "Here."

"Oh, I…I didn't see your hand. Sorry." He took the phone from her. *Of course you didn't see it you moron. You were ogling her thighs.*

20

3

HE'D SEEN HER BUTT EARLIER, NOW HE WAS STARING AT HER thigh. Next, he would want to feel her up. Well, that wouldn't be so bad—those big, strong hands. But was she safe? Since her father sent him, she believed he would only look and not touch. Not that he looked on purpose. Each time, she'd put herself on display. But damn, he was HOT.

It had rained off and on, but the journey seemed to be never-ending. Just getting out of Georgia seemed to take forever. He spoke and broke her thoughts.

"Let me know when you're tired of my songs. We can play anything you want."

"It's fine. As long as you keep it that low." She felt a burning sensation like he was staring at her and turned to look. Yep, he was looking.

"I'm dying of curiosity. I have two questions. Your dad said you were attacked. What happened?"

Priyanka told him. She'd gone for a walk and her phone and handbag were stolen.

"Good thing we're driving. It would have been hard to get on a plane without an ID or police report. So why didn't you report to the police?"

"I was scared. It's a small town. Everybody knows everybody. What if one of the attackers was the son of the police chief? They would try to cover it up by making me disappear."

Mason laughed. "You've been watching a lot of TV shows. But it's plausible."

Priyanka felt herself loosening up, warming up to him. "What about you?"

"Oh, oh, what about me?"

She giggled. "I hear some Boston in you."

"I grew up in a small town in Maine. Went to college in Cambridge Mass."

"Really. Where?" She curled her legs under her. "Don't tell me Harvard. That was my parents' wish for me. I disappointed them. They would love you."

"No, I went to MIT."

"That's good enough. I went to Boston University. Got a BFA—"

Mason turned to her. "Best Friends Always…who's the lucky guy?"

Priyanka punched him playfully on the arm and laughed. "You have jokes, eh? It's a Bachelor of Fine Arts."

They both laughed.

"Wow that's great. I respect creativity. Are you any good?"

Priyanka shrugged. "Art is subjective—a labor of love." She paused for a moment. "Depending on how this trip ends, I'll make you one, then you decide."

"It's okay, but you don't have to. My second question is—"

"Why I ran away from home?"

"Mm-hmm. Let me put some popcorn in the microwave," said Mason. "This is going to be an interesting movie."

"Do you have any Indian friends?"

"Of course. Raj, Ajay, Preeti, Kavita, and now Sanjay."

Priyanka chuckled. "My dad?"

Mason nodded.

"Okay, impressive. Anyway, in India, most of the time marriages are arranged. The parents do the arranging. My father was doing his emergency medicine residency in Boston when my mother was arranged by my grandparents and sent."

Mason grinned. "Like a blind date? Or mail order bride?"

Priyanka waggled her head, weighing what to say. "Mmm…in the broader sense, yes. But a lot goes into it. Both families work together to make it happen."

"So why did you decide to go MIA?"

"MIA. Missing in action?"

"Yep," said Mason.

"Well, it starts with a date. But that's not my main problem. I have contracts to produce artwork, and I'm barely able to be on schedule. Despite telling my mom to back off, she comes into my studio every now and then with a 'This will only take a second. What do you think of this ad?' By the time she's done, I have to recollect my thoughts before I can pick up from where I left off. If I miss deadlines regularly, I'll become known as the artist that can't keep a deadline, and the jobs will dry up."

"That's tough. I have a friend who's a writer. She complains about that too. Her family is always dropping in asking for this or that. And when she tells them she's working, they'll say 'You just sit, stare at the screen, then type. That's not work.'"

"Exactly. People don't understand. Or don't want to understand. In my own case, it's a dinner date with me, my parents, and the guy at our house. You guys might not like each other. But your parents…the two families already think it's a good match, so there's a lot of pressure on you to make it work." She shook her head. "I tried a few, but it didn't work. It's not my thing. I told them to stop. Especially my mother, but…"

"Wow, that's a lot of pressure." Mason was quiet for some time, then he shook his head. "Well, I guess I can imagine my mother introducing me to her friends' daughters. 'This is Emily. She works at Goldman Sachs in New York. You guys should exchange numbers and meet up for lunch or something.' Mason mimicked an older woman's voice. "Maybe I'll meet for the…or something."

Priyanka threw her head back and laughed. "What is it with guys and sex? You make a lot of noise about getting some. Then you get in there, pump for one minute if you're any good, then the next minute you're shaking like a car that blew its front tires, then it's all over. Over for the guy that is, while the girl is just getting started." She covered her hands with her face. "Oh God. I'm so embarrassed I said that. I don't even know you."

"Well, I know you. And I'm confident I'd recognize your ass anywhere."

She smiled and shook her head. "You're crazy."

She wondered if she'd taken it too far in such a short time.

He glanced at her, then faced the road. "That's…that's a very good analogy—the one about the blown front tire. I mean the vibration. That was exactly how it felt inside the plane this morning, just that I had the opposite of a climax."

Priyanka snorted laughter. It was so easy talking to him.

They drove on in companionable silence for a few miles. The playlist cut off at intervals to advertise that people should not forget to get their flowers and chocolate for the people they loved.

"At this rate, you think we'll get there tomorrow?" asked Priyanka.

"It's Valentine's Day. We have to."

Priyanka felt a stab of jealousy. "Oh, we have plans? A significant other?"

"Ah…it's an appointment."

An appointment on Valentine's Day? It could only be with a girl. Why doesn't he come out and say he has a girlfriend? Or maybe he doesn't have.

"Okay, Priyanka, I'm not trying to flog a dead horse here, but you've run away before…"

"Psst, it's not running away." She turned and looked out of her window. "It's more like taking time off. Especially when the guy wants to visit again. A second look around like I'm an open house. Hoping maybe I'll see them in a better light. Or they come to flaunt their wealth." She exhaled noisily. "So if I know they're coming, I'll just make myself scarce."

"Ah, okay, that explains it. Maybe you have to explain to your parents how you feel."

Priyanka let out a sarcastic laugh. "My dad is cool about it, but my mom—I know she wants the best for me. Sometimes I wish I had a sibling, a sister to spread the pressure around." She looked down at her hands folded in her lap. Was she baring her soul to this guy?

"I feel your pain. Maybe talk to your parents some…"

She looked up when he stopped talking. Mason cut out of the right lane and got onto the speed lane to pass an 18-wheeler. Priyanka held her breath. It seemed to take forever to overtake these huge trucks on the highway. The truck's engine rumbled like thunder when they were next to it. Eventually, they passed it and settled in a comfortable distance and pace in front of it. Her eyes went back to her lap.

Mason exhaled. "As I was saying, things could get dangerous, like what happened in Georgia. I don't blame the guys that come back trying to impress you. You are great company. You're…you're beautiful. Heck, you're HOT. I would act the same way if I were in their shoes."

Priyanka's head shot up. She looked at him. Did he just use beautiful and hot to refer to her? She stared at him and felt her pulse start to race.

Mason turned and looked at her. "What?"

She gazed into his eyes, long and deep. Her eyes not leaving him, she leaned forward, brushed her lips against his, then kissed him. Priyanka closed her eyes as a sudden rush of heat spread from her groin outward.

He kissed her back, his tongue probing her mouth.

Her heartbeat pounded so hard in her chest she could feel it in her whole body. In fact, it was shaking the entire car.

Priyanka's eyes flew open to the blast of a truck horn. They almost popped out of their sockets. Hurtling closer and closer to them was the 18-wheeler.

4

MASON

MASON BROKE OFF THE KISS AND TURNED THE WHEEL A little to the right. Ahead of them, the truck's co-passenger stuck his head out of the window, and his lips clearly said, 'Get a room.'

Priyanka grimaced and bit her lower lip. "I'm really sorry. I don't know what made me do that. I nearly got us killed."

"No, you didn't. I already saw the truck in the rearview mirror." His eyes darted to her, then back to the road. *Look at those lips.* God, she was beautiful. How could he get her to do that again? Mason knew he was in trouble. He now wanted her. In his mind's eye, he could see her climbing down from the hotel balcony, her round butt in clear view. That image was seared in his mind. It was now the go-to image for the next time he jerked off. Now he was getting the mother of all erections.

She turned to look at him. "How far do we have to go?"

Her gaze felt like fire on his skin. That kiss had changed

everything and shown him a bigger picture for the two of them. Whispering naughty suggestions into his ear. "We still have a long way, but we should stop and get some food, stretch our legs, and…pee. I don't know about you, but I have a full tank."

"Now that you've mentioned it, I'll need to tinkle too."

Mason swallowed. An image of what he imagined her swollen pussy would look like flashed through his mind. He opened his mouth to speak but couldn't string any words together. "Mm-hmm."

"You're now my personal Dr. Phil. That's what happens when you're stuck in a car with a guy for four hours."

"You have any preference for where to stop?" He tapped the screen of his phone. "We have a few options. The Golden—"

"The closest will be fine."

Mason pulled into a Gas N Grub and drove to the fuel pumps. "Why don't you go in? I'll buy gas, then come meet you inside."

"Sure." She exited the car.

He watched her walk toward the entrance, his eyes glued to her ass. *Dude, she's off-limits. She's a client's daughter. This is Business 101:* Don't get high on your own supply. *In this case, if you mess around with the product and the word gets around, no one will trust you with business.* But she'd started it. What business did she have kissing him?

The fuel pump clicked.

His tank was full. Mason closed the tank, took his receipt, and got back into the car. He drove to the convenience store. Once inside, he looked around for Priyanka.

"Hey." She waved and smiled at him from the confectionery stand.

Mason's heart missed a beat again. She must have freshened up. Just like the first time he saw her in the hotel. She was so beautiful. He walked over to her.

"What do you want? They have everything. Burgers, hot dogs, pizza, make your own sandwich—whatever."

She flashed those big round eyes at him and caught him looking at her with lust in his eyes.

She batted her eyelids and looked down. When she looked up, her nostrils flared. "So what would it be?"

"Just get me a hotdog and two burgers, plus whatever sandwich you're concocting for yourself."

"Can you handle hot and spicy?"

Oh God. All he could think of was sitting in the backseat of the Pathfinder and Priyanka straddling him with his cock buried deep in her tight little pussy. Mason nodded and headed for the bathroom. Then he turned and came back. He fished out his wallet and handed her his credit card. "There's a line in the bathroom. In case I'm not out when it gets to you."

By the time Mason came out, she was waiting for him with plastic bags of their food and drink.

"They have a seating area," said Mason. "Do you want to sit and eat?"

She pursed her lips and thought for a second. "Remember you have an appointment on Valentine's Day. The sooner we get there, the better for you."

Mason's breath caught. He let out a nervous laugh. "No, it's not what you think." He was tempted to tell her the whole Cupid Cabana thing and his grandfather's will, but that would be making himself out to be a loser with women. "We'll get there. I prefer getting a good night's sleep rather than driving all night and barely awake in the morning. Let's eat here."

"Sleeping well will make you a more focused driver in the morning," said Priyanka.

29

Mason started with the hotdog. She'd been upfront with him about herself. Maybe he should share too. "The reason I'm rushing back for Valentine's Day isn't what you think."

"It's not? You don't have a significant other waiting?"

He shook his head. "No." He then told her about the will.

"I thought I had issues, but this is crazy." She put down her sandwich and wiped her lips with a napkin. "You have to get engaged before the end of this month? Then married a year after February?"

"Yes, and I can't just get any random girl because they'll say yes and hang in for the ride. And after the marriage they get a divorce, grab half of the money, and go without producing a baby."

Priyanka cocked her head. "A baby?"

"Yes. Well, at least remain married for a year, plus or minus the baby."

"There are women out there who will do that."

"Maybe, but I don't have time. Imagine I came up to you and made you that proposal that we must be engaged by the end of the month and married in twelve."

"Stranger danger," said Priyanka in a sing-song voice. "Throw in pervert too."

Mason laughed. "Exactly."

She sat back in her chair, exhaled, then picked up her sandwich. Then she put it down and took a long drink from her orange juice. "I think we can help each other out."

Mason's eyebrows narrowed. "How?" He took a bite of the hot dog.

"My mother is a big fan of matrimonial ads, and we can game the system."

Mason stopped chewing. He raised an eyebrow and cocked his head. "Did you say matrimonial ads?"

Priyanka gave him an incredulous stare as if he'd just

asked if fish could survive in water. "Of course. Indian parents use it a lot. You put an ad in the newspaper of the type of guy or girl you want for your child."

Mason put down his burger. "No way."

"Yes way."

"Tell me more."

"We put out a fake matrimonial ad with all the attributes my mom likes. She'll gravitate to it and pick it. Naturally, she'll show me, I'll accept it, and we'll get engaged." Priyanka pointed at herself. "What's in it for me? I get my parents off my back to paint and not fall back on my schedule. For you, your inheritance is secured."

"I don't really understand matrimonial ads, but say we do that, what happens at the end of the year? When we're supposed to get married?"

Priyanka shrugged. "We get married and know it's a one-year commitment. At the end of that year, you have your inheritance, and I'm well established in my career, then we go our separate ways. No harm, no foul. Our secret is intact."

"What about the baby?"

"Minus a baby, of course. Not everybody gets pregnant in their first year of marriage." Priyanka flushed. "Not that we would be trying."

Mason stuffed the rest of the hot dog into his mouth and thought as he chewed. What could go wrong with this? They both had reasons to maintain secrecy. He swallowed. "I'm beginning to like it."

Priyanka spread out her hands. "I think it's a great idea. We'll just have some ground rules. Because we'll be engaged, there'll be kissing and public display of affection, but no sex."

"No sex?"

"Of course no sex. You can get that where you normally get it now."

His eyes were on her lips. Heat surged through his body, and he felt his jeans getting tight. She indeed had a way with words. Mason took a bite of his sandwich, the same ingredients as the one Priyanka had made for herself, and started to chew. He felt they were missing something but couldn't place a finger on it. "It's delicious!" he said through a mouthful.

She nodded. "I'm glad you like it."

He swallowed, then took another bite. Then he felt the heat. He must have chewed a raw ghost pepper because his mouth started to burn. It felt like someone had tossed a grenade into his mouth and pinched it shut. Mason sprinted to the garbage and spat the food into it.

Priyanka followed him with a bottle of orange juice. "Are you okay?"

"I think so!" He coughed then took a long drink from the orange juice.

"I thought you said you could handle hot and spicy?" She placed a hand behind his neck and stroked him.

He didn't want to say he thought she was referring to her body. "Kind of. But it feels like someone swapped the vinegar for gasoline."

Priyanka giggled. "Sorry. Okay, okay. That wasn't funny. Hold on, let me get you a bottle of milk. Continue to rinse with the orange juice." She ran off into the store.

By the time she came back with an eight-ounce bottle of milk, Mason felt a lot better. They sat back down together.

"I'll just eat the burgers," said Mason and pried the bun open. Satisfied, he closed it, took a bite, and chewed. "Okay, let's do it."

Her eyes danced and sparkled. "Are you sure?" She sounded bubbly.

"No, but it seems to be the only viable option."

"Yay!" Priyanka's hands shot up in the air. Then she took his half-eaten sandwich and started to eat it without any discomfort.

His eyes widened, not believing the pepper had zero effect on her.

"This is good. I did well with the combination of peppers and veggies."

"Did you undergo some kind of training on how to eat dynamite?"

She laughed. "I've always had hot peppers in my food since I was a kid." She chuckled. "We'll never be compatible in the matrimonial ads if we include food."

"Let's talk more in the car and maybe set up the ad when we crash for the night. I want us to be at least halfway into the trip before we stop."

"Sounds good," said Priyanka. "This is turning out to be the best road trip ever."

5

PRIYANKA

"So the ads are placed in an Indian newspaper in India?" asked Mason as they cruised along the highway. "In physical newspapers?"

"Yes. My mother is the expert on this. Initially, I was intrigued by the process the first time she showed it to me. I wondered why they used actual newspapers. Online would be more efficient."

"Yes, why not?"

"The explanation I got was anybody could go online, upload a picture, and place an ad for cheap or even free. But with the newspapers, it costs between fifty and a hundred dollars, which is a lot in India. So it attracts only serious people. Also, it doesn't have pictures. Without pictures, fickle young people don't bother. But parents who love to dig into family backgrounds and horoscope compatibility take a harder look."

"Is your mom mad with you for going MIA? I mean after all the effort she put in."

"I guess. Every now and then, Mother invites someone to the house. She's put a lot of work into it. You need your phone for navigation, but when we stop for the night, I'll show you some of these ads."

After a few moments of silence, Mason said, "But since she's here in the States, how does she place the ads?"

"She has an account with a broker. For a fee, they do the legwork. They go to the newspaper's office and place ads in Mumbai or wherever."

Even though it was her idea, Priyanka felt scared that it might not turn out as planned. Maybe she should have put some more thought into it. They drove for another two hours before Mason said they should find a place to spend the night. Darkness had crept in, and driving does take its toll.

Mason tapped the phone screen, selected the lodging icon. Minutes later, they exited the highway. After a few stop signs, lights, and turns, they pulled into a hotel not too far from the highway.

"Looks decent enough," said Mason. "The parking lot is almost full, so we're not the lone star in the galaxy that thinks it's a great hotel."

Priyanka walked behind Mason and watched him as they headed for the receptionist's counter. There was something about him she liked. Would she date him if he asked her out? Maybe, but it would just be a fling. But they were way ahead. They were now talking engagement in two weeks and marriage in a year.

He was white, she was Indian. It had just occurred to her that if he showed up at her house as her match, it wouldn't go down well. A shudder ran down Priyanka's spine. Her mother would blow a fuse. She didn't think his parents would be overjoyed, either. But a one-night stand could work.

She'd never been that adventurous. Maybe since she was already on an adventure, she might as well check off her bucket list. *What bucket list? You don't even have one.* Exactly—that's why she wasn't going to act on it.

"Well, we have only one room left," said the receptionist.

The woman's voice brought her back to the present. "W-what did you say?"

Mason turned to her. "They have only one room left." He looked at the receptionist. "Maybe someone will cancel."

"Not very likely. Most of the time, the guests are just minutes away when they make the reservation."

"We'll take it!" said Priyanka.

Mason turned to look at her. "Are you sure? We can find another hotel."

She shook her head. "You're tired. I'm tired…"

Mason nodded at the lady.

The receptionist smiled and collected Mason's information. Then her phone rang. "Excuse me, please."

Priyanka looked around the lobby and noticed they had an outdoor eating arraignment with outdoor heaters.

"Would you like to check that out?" asked Mason. He nodded in the direction of the outdoor tables.

"I need a shower first, then I'm ready for anything."

The receptionist hung up. "You're in luck. This rarely happens. A second room just came up. Someone canceled. It's a king—"

"Yes!" said Mason and pumped his fist. "We'll take it." He completed the forms, collected the keys, and gave one to Priyanka. "Why don't you go ahead? I'll see if they have anything I could wear in the hotel's store. Meet down here in fifteen, for food or cocktails?"

"That's true." She slapped her forehead. "I keep forgetting this was supposed to be a few hours' trip for you. You didn't pack anything. Let's meet in twenty."

"Dress to kill."

When Priyanka came down twenty-five minutes later dressed in a short red dress that stopped just above the knee, she found Mason on the patio wearing a black T-shirt printed with a white silhouette Virginia map over his blue jeans. He looked fresh and relaxed. That fluttery feeling returned to her stomach.

His face lit up when he saw her. "I'm not hitting on you, but each time I see you, your beauty hits me on the head like a sledgehammer."

"Hmmm, flattery. You know what they say about that."

Mason stood up and pulled out a chair for her. "No, what?"

"Be careful what you unleash. It might be too hot to handle."

"I'll cross that bridge when we get to it. I was thirsty and got some Hennessey and Coke. What would you like to drink?"

"Sex on the beach." *Where did that come from?* Priyanka couldn't believe how flirtatious she was. This was dangerous territory.

Mason grinned and called for the waiter. "I'll order something light. I'm not really that hungry. I need to sleep well."

About forty minutes later, they'd finished eating and were on their second drink for Mason and third for Priyanka when they returned to matrimonial ads and their plan.

"So if you're young, short, and not well educated," said Mason, "your horoscope is shit, and you're pushing burgers somewhere in Mumbai, you're essentially fucked? No wife for you?" He cocked his head.

"Well, not exactly. I believe there's a guy for every girl and vice versa. They just might have a hard time finding each other."

"Hmm, that's deep. But I think there are some good parts too to the matrimonial ad approach."

"Like what?" said Priyanka, a slight slur to her voice.

"Well, if the romance starts after marriage, then the couple has a longer time to enjoy the relationship before the novelty wears off."

"If you say so. Anyway, it's time we solidified our plans. Mr. Mason Sutton, are you ready for your first matrimonial ad?"

"Yes."

"Give me your phone."

He handed it to her.

Priyanka tapped and typed on the screen. She set up an account with the broker, used one of the payment systems saved on his phone to pay for the service, and it was ready for ads. She exhaled. "Here we go. How tall are you?"

"Six feet two inches."

"How tall do you want your wife to be?"

"Just like you."

"Okay, five feet eight. Very good. You're learning fast."

"What else?" asked Mason.

She spoke as she typed. "So handsome male twenty-eight-year-old MIT graduate seeks beautiful bride twenty-four to twenty-six. Well settled—means has a job. Issueless or does not have kids." She stopped typing and looked at him. "Will you marry outside your caste…your race?"

"I would."

"Any negatives? Like you'd prefer a non-Facebook user. Your potential mate can wear pants in the home, but once they step outside must wear a dress or sari."

"Okay, I trust your selection on that."

"Any professions you would rather they don't apply?"

"Of course. My ex was a computer engineer. We spent a great deal of time talking about computers and planning for the future. But she was only waiting for a payday."

"What about horoscope compatibility?"

Mason's eyebrows shot up. "Horoscope compatibility?"

"For my mom, horoscope compatibility must be on point. Anything less than twenty, you get a rejection right away."

"So how do we fix that? We don't want the whole thing to fall through."

Priyanka shook her head. "That's our Achilles heel. If it fails, then the whole system crumbles."

Mason was quiet. He took a long drink from his glass. "Then it better not fail."

"I'll drink to that." Priyanka almost drained her glass. "Good thing I'm not driving. I'm getting buzzed."

"Wow, this is fascinating. I'm beginning to believe in the merits of the system."

"You think Twitter's 140 characters is restrictive, these ads cram a lot in. They do more with fewer characters." Priyanka made some final adjustments. "All right. I think I have your ad ready. Here, take a look."

Mason looked at the screen.

H'som 6 2" groom 28 MIT grad W'stld.
Seeks B'ful bride 5 8", 24-26 W'stld & I'less.
Caste no bar. Horoscope compatibility a MUST.
(Software engineers kindly do not apply)

. . .

Mason laughed. "This is like reading the periodic table. Are you sure they'll understand the abbreviations?"

Priyanka chuckled. "This is as easy as it gets. There's PQ—professionally qualified, Conv ED—convent educated for girls, PA—Per Annum, T'tot—"

"Is that a type of toy for toddlers?"

Priyanka banged her palm on the table and laughed. "Oh God," she said, still laughing. "I think I just peed my panties." When her laughter subsided, she said, "A teetotaler is a person who doesn't drink. That's not the two of us."

"Why don't they just write that? A person who doesn't drink."

"Remember, limited space." She sniffed the air. "I think rain is on the way." A few drops landed on the table. More could be heard on rooftops not far away. "It's going to get heavier. Let's get out of here." She picked up her drink and drained it.

Mason did the same, then put his phone away. "This way!" He ran into a small indent in the wall and pulled her in close against his body.

In front of them, the rain came down heavily, touching her feet. Heat swept through her. Something hard pressed against her butt. Priyanka laughed. "That better be your cell phone."

Behind her, Mason's breathing grew faster and urgent.

She pushed her butt against him and felt the pressure from his cock.

Mason gasped, and his hot breath behind her neck fired off a jolt of sweetness all the way to her pussy.

Mason let out a deep moan and pulled her tighter, grinding his cock into her.

Priyanka raised her head, shuddering as his lips brushed against her ears. A fluttery sensation started in her chest and spread down to her stomach. Her pussy tingled and throbbed. His hands slid down and squeezed her crotch through her dress, setting her on fire. Her whole body shivered with desire.

"Let's get out of here," said Mason, breathing hard. His voice was tight with want.

She giggled and ran into the rain, pulling him along. They crashed through the door into the reception area, giggling like teenagers. "Come on, let's go dry off." Priyanka walked over to the elevator. Her pulse raced like a horse spooked by the backfire of a car's exhaust. She felt alive, ready to fuck him on the ride inside the elevator.

Another couple joined them, and that was the only thing that stopped her from jumping him. They got off on the second floor. She led the way to her room. Priyanka inserted the key card, pulled it out, and they were in.

As soon as the door clicked shut behind them, she was against him. This was thirst, a deep-seated craving that needed to be quenched. She'd wanted to drink him in the moment she saw him at the hotel. She didn't plan on marrying him. She didn't need her mother's or anyone else's approval to mount him. She slammed her lips against his. Heat and want cascaded through her, setting off a flood between her legs.

He responded, giving as good as he got. Their tongues intertwined. His hard cock pressed against her body.

Mason pulled back, his chest rising and falling, a wild look in his eyes as if begging her to pull them back from a line they were about to cross. They needed to think this through. He tried to delay it. "That's a nice dress you have on. I've been wondering all night what's underneath it."

"Nobody's stopping you from finding out."

He raised his hand, palm facing her. "Are you sure?"

She stepped forward, grabbed a fistful of his T-shirt, and yanked him closer. She brushed her lips against his and ran her hands over his chest. "I need to see what's under your shirt. Take it off."

In a flurry of movement, Mason had his T-shirt over his head and tossed to the side.

She ran her hand over his chest, soft at first, then deeper, feeling the hard muscles underneath. "You take care of yourself."

"I do what I can."

She stroked his nipples.

He cupped her ass.

Her lips crashed into his. Her hands went around his neck, and her legs wound around his waist.

Mason was lucky he was steady on his feet. His palms wrapped around her butt, and he held them up as he staggered to the bed. Their lips separated once they landed on the sheets.

She raised her hand. "Take them off me." She kicked her shoes off, and they landed on the floor with a thud.

"Priyanka." It sounded like a warning.

The way her name came off his tongue fired her off even more.

He grabbed the hem of the little red dress and pulled it up, his eyes getting wider and wider as each new succulent part of her body was exposed.

"Priyanka."

6

MASON

A SHAKY BREATH SHOT OUT OF MASON. HER BODY WAS A sight to behold. Full, round, real breasts wrapped in a black lacy bra. Her stomach was flat, and her crotch covered with the tiniest piece of lace he'd ever seen. "Wow, look at that."

"Is looking all you want to do?"

"Jesus." His jeans got tighter. Her words were like an aphrodisiac, urging him on. Mason ran his hands over the top of her breast and watched as goosebumps appeared all over her skin. He dipped his hands under the cups of her bra. Greedily he filled his hands with her breasts and squeezed. "God, you feel amazing in my hands."

She moaned.

His fingers found her nipples and rolled them to hardness, ready for his lips and tongue. Mason nibbled and sucked each nipple. He was not disappointed. They tasted like honey.

Breathless, she gripped his hair with both fists. "I wanted you the first time I set eyes on you. We have to finish this.

43

You must finish this." She kissed him hard. Then she pulled back.

Mason had been on perpetual edge since he'd met her. The molten look in her eyes and the words from her lips were like gasoline on a blazing flame. Heat surged through him. He kissed her fiercely.

Priyanka unbuckled his belt and undid his jeans button. She traced a finger along his exposed skin.

He shivered as if touched by hot and cold metal. Her fingers set off little fires where they landed. He heard his zipper come down. He wriggled his hips to help as her hands dragged his jeans halfway down his thighs.

She wrapped her hand around his cock and gasped. "So thick…so big."

Mason shuddered. He prayed to all the deities he could think of that he didn't explode in her hand. He had to take control. "Tell me what you want, and I'll give it to you."

She lowered herself on the bed, resting on her elbows.

He followed and brushed his lips against hers.

"I want you inside me, Mason." Her impatient hands were everywhere. One second, one hand was on his butt, pushing him closer. The next, her hand nudged his cock against her core.

He pushed forward. "Like this? You want me to take you like this?" He thrust his hips forward and rocked against her, pressing his cock harder against the fabric of her panties, demonstrating how he would take her.

Her breath caught, and she whimpered, "Yes."

Her voice was so sexy. It nearly ended for Mason right there. He reached down, pushed her thong aside, and slid a finger in. She was dripping. He nuzzled at her breasts, sucked each nipple, then went up to her neck.

He took her lips, tasting the vodka and orange juice. All

this time, his fingers were not resting. He worked them hard. First one, then two fingers, in and out of her wet pussy. Faster and faster trying to bring her closer to the edge before he mounted her.

Priyanka writhed and moaned, thrusting her hips forward to meet his fingers. "Deeper, faster." It was a demand.

Mason's finger could only go so deep. He pulled his hand out and lowered himself on top of her.

She spread her legs wider, grabbed his cock, and went to work. She rubbed the tip against her pussy lips, massaged her clit, then positioned it in the center. She was more than ready. "Yes Mason, right now."

With a thrust of hips, he was inside her. His lips quivered as he tried to put what he felt into words. All he managed was gibberish. He drew back and plunged back in, letting out a satisfied moan.

"Yes, so good. Faster…deeper." Her hands on his butt urged him forward. She raised her hips to meet him, and they fucked like rabbits, racing to satisfy the sexual tension coming to a crescendo inside them.

He pumped and ground into her.

She matched him stroke for stroke, leaving him breathless. Mason gasped. "Jesus, Pri…Where…where have you been hiding this pussy?" Right now, he straddled the edge of ecstasy. It felt so good. He wanted to prolong it. Make it last longer.

"Don't…don't come yet."

"I can't…hold…"

"I'm…I'm almost there with—"

Mason, too, was at the point of no return.

Priyanka never finished that sentence.

Mason felt her pussy tighten around his cock like a vise.

She stopped moving. Her long legs, wrapped around his

hips, locked him in place. Priyanka began to whimper. The deep well of sexual passion deep inside her bubbled to the surface like a spring. She let out a scream.

The sound of her voice was all it took to push him over. Mason let go with a roar. He released the barrage of fire he'd been trying to hold on to. His body trembled as his balls pumped load after load into her. Her screams of ecstasy mixed with his. He collapsed on her, sweaty and trembling.

7

PRIYANKA

PRIYANKA BLINKED, THEN SHUT HER EYES. SUNLIGHT streaming in through the edges of the curtain had woken her. She opened her eyes and shielded her face with her hand.

It took her a moment to realize where she was. She was naked, her head nestled on Mason's chest. She listened to his soft snores and watched the gentle rise and fall of his chest as he slept. The smell of sex was all around her, drawing her thoughts to last night.

After their first orgasm, the hotel room phone had started to ring as they lay in each other's arms soaked with sweat. It was the receptionist trying to confirm they were all right. Another guest had called that it sounded like someone was getting murdered in the room next to theirs. Mason assured her they were fine, but she demanded to speak with Priyanka too. Only after speaking with her was she satisfied.

Priyanka had never let herself go like that before. The

orgasm was well worth it. It was no strings attached sex, and so far, she had no regrets. Was that how one-night stands felt? Mason was a nice guy, but that was where it should end. Trying to imagine the look on her mother's face if she showed up with Mason as a potential mate sent shivers down her spine. Then she remembered their plan and knew they'd crossed a line even before starting.

She stared at Mason, feasting on his naked body. He had his elbow over his eyes, one leg dangled over the bed, and the big cock between his legs stood like the Washington Monument. Dang. How did she get that inside her?

She took her time to enjoy his muscular body. Other times she'd had sex, it was always under cloak of darkness. As she watched him, that fluttery warm feeling spread from her stomach to her throbbing pussy. She'd always wondered what it would be like to have a cock at her disposal to ride as she wanted.

Whether Mason's erection was from dreaming about sex or morning wood, she was mounting him and riding to her satisfaction.

Priyanka didn't give it much thought. She was soaked and ready. She straddled him and exhaled as her pussy engulfed him. She closed her eyes and lifted her hips sliding up, then down on his cock. For several precious moments, it was just her alone enjoying the ride.

Then Mason cupped her ass, raised her up, and slammed her down on his cock.

"You read my mind," said Mason. "Nothing beats an early morning fuck." He moaned. "Oh yes. That feels so good."

She slapped his hands away. "Please keep your hands to yourself and no screaming."

Mason chuckled. Not opening his eyes, he nodded and rested his head on his intertwined fingers.

Gradually her tempo increased. Muffled moans and groans came from her and Mason as they tried to keep quiet. She placed her hands on his chest for support as she sped up and slowed down at her leisure, taking her pleasure.

Soon, she began the journey up the hill, reaching for that deep pleasure. Her breathing came in gasps. Her focus was on riding his cock, slamming her pussy down on it, filling the room with the *flup flup flup* sound of his hard cock sliding in and out of her wetness.

All her nerve endings were firing as one, chasing that one final signal to get her over the edge. Coherent thought wasn't part of what she was experiencing.

"Almost there," she said breathlessly. The fluttery feeling in her abdomen became a wave that exploded outward to every part of her body. She came and came.

Mason grabbed her butt. He pushed his hips up, sliding his cock deeper into her. Muffled sounds of pleasure rumbled out of him.

Priyanka felt his cock get bigger inside her, then erupt like a volcano.

His fingers dug into her butt, holding on for dear life as he came. Her name stuck on his lips.

She collapsed on his chest, a quivering mess.

Mason stroked her hair, whispering sweet nothings in her ear as she got her breath back.

Priyanka realized something was different. She'd crossed a line she didn't know existed when a good fuck brought out emotions that didn't exist before. Things that were not supposed to happen.

Feeling shy suddenly, she rushed to the bathroom, turning

once to catch a glimpse of him. No, she couldn't be developing feelings for him. He lay on the bed, stretched out like Leonardo da Vinci's Vitruvian man. His semi-hard thick penis, glistening with their juices, rested on his stomach.

Priyanka cleaned up, brushed her teeth, then got into the shower. This had to end right here. They had to just stick to the original plan. She would talk to him. They'd had their fun. It was now time to move on. Despite what she felt was the right thing to do, she wondered if he had feelings for her. Could one have mind-blowing sex without an emotional connection?

Priyanka got out of the shower and toweled herself dry. She picked up the complimentary lotion in the bathroom and read the label. It was good enough. She put some on her palm and heard Mason's phone ring in the bedroom. Her ears pricked up when she heard Mason say, *Dr. Patel*. She listened.

"Good morning, Sanjay. We're about halfway. Stopped at Virginia for the night. At the most, we should be in Beaver Run in the next six to seven hours."

Pause.

"Oh, Priyanka? She's in her room. I…I'm meeting her for breakfast in ten minutes. I can have her call you."

Pause.

"My fee? We're still on the road. I'll send you an invoice as soon as we get back. Just in case we incur more expenses."

Pause.

"I'll do that, sir—sorry, Sanjay. Bye-bye."

Sadness washed over Priyanka. She'd known he was getting paid. It was his job. But to hear the enthusiasm in his voice meant that what happened had meant nothing to him. It was all about his fees and his inheritance. The sex was the icing on the cake for him. She took a deep breath and let it out through her nose.

She couldn't back away now. The plan was still solid. They would both get what they wanted, nothing more and nothing less. The sooner she stopped harboring any thoughts of what could be, the better for them.

8

MASON

MASON COULDN'T BELIEVE HOW THINGS HAD GONE DOWNHILL
so fast. In the grand scheme of things, it was for the better.
But he'd thought that after the night they'd spent together,
they had something good going. Priyanka told him during
breakfast in no uncertain terms that she'd caved to the stress
from the past few days.

"What happened between us was a way for the body to
get rid of tension," she'd said. "I just survived a robbery. You
escaped unscathed from a plane crash." She moved her food
around her plate. "I don't think it's something we should let
happen again."

Mason picked his words carefully. With her, he felt something different. There had been a real connection, and the sex
had been mind-blowing. He was scared to explore it and
cautious to dismiss it. His last girlfriend had cheated on him.
He'd gone to surprise her and drop off her favorite lunch and
ended up being the one surprised. He'd found her leaning on

a computer tower, her skirt wrapped around her waist and her business partner working with gusto behind her.

"There might be nothing there, but don't you think it's something we—"

"It was a mistake. We have cultural differences and other deep-seated baggage that would be an impediment to a future together. It's futile trying…"

Mason nodded slowly and took a sip of his coffee. He'd woken up to the most glorious fuck of his life. Now he was confused by the turn of events. Granted, it was a relatively brief interlude between meeting, getting to know each other, and ending up in bed, but it'd followed a natural progression. It wasn't contrived in any way. Insta love, they called it. Then they had the fake matrimonial ad thing too.

Now barely an hour later after that glorious early morning sex, he was getting the cold shoulder from her. Were the events of last night and this morning a dream? Like it never happened.

"But between when you took a shower and now, did I do anything that pissed you off?"

She let out a nervous laugh. Her eyes darted to him, then away. "That's what I'm saying. It was all stress. We got rid of it, but it would probably build back up. By then, we should have gone our separate ways."

"But remember we're supposed to keep up appearances once the matrimonial ad kicks in."

Priyanka slapped her forehead as if suddenly developing a headache. "Did you send it out?"

"Last night, after I read it and the rains came, I hit send."

She groaned. "You know we didn't think it through. We missed a major part. I'm Indian, expected to marry an Indian boy. You're white. I'm sure your parents won't be jumping for joy when you show up with me. And your grandfather that came up with that ridiculous will, I can't fathom what his position would be."

That's what he was missing too, thought Mason. "Well, it's still a solid plan. We both get what we want. I'm sure we'll figure something out."

Priyanka sighed. "Okay."

He nodded slowly. He would respect her wishes. After breakfast, they hit the highway, and things went from bad to worse. Priyanka reclined the seat and shut her eyes. He couldn't really tell if she was sleeping or not. She only opened them when the phone rang, and it was her father.

Mason apologized for not calling earlier. He gave the phone to Priyanka. She had a good talk with her father, but it was like listening to two enemies trying to be cordial when her mother came on.

Well, thought Mason. He wasn't the only one getting the cold treatment. "Do you mind if I listen to an audio-book?"

She turned, gave him a halfhearted smile, and shook her head. Then she closed her eyes again.

"Thank you," said Mason and tapped the screen. Soon the narration for *A Tale of Two Cities* started to play.

They made a few stops for gas and food. The stops were strictly business. Buy gas, use the bathroom, buy food, and move on. It was a far cry from the first time they'd stopped.

At the last gas station, Mason bought some chocolate bars and a small box of assorted chocolate. He'd planned on giving it to her but didn't know what she would say or do. So he held back.

They made good time. Maybe because they didn't spend too much time at stops. On I-95 in Delaware, Mason decided to give her the box of chocolates since the trip would be over soon. He unclipped his seat belt, stretched to the back seat, and retrieved it.

"Priyanka?"

"Mm-hmm."

"For you." He thrust the square box, bound with a red ribbon, toward her. On the cover were pictures of the contents, assorted chocolate.

She turned.

"Happy Valentine's Day."

Her eyebrows narrowed, then her eyes widened.

Mason didn't expect her to be surprised.

"Oh, thank you!" She took the box. "Now I feel like a douche. Sorry I didn't get you anything."

"That's okay. It's nothing much."

"It's the thought that matters." She opened the box. "It has coconut and milk chocolate." She squealed with delight. "My favorite. This is the real deal." She kissed him on the cheek, then plucked one and tossed it into her mouth.

Mason eyed the box just to make sure it wasn't drugs he'd picked up by mistake. He couldn't understand women. Just like that, her mood changed. He'd try not to upset her.

They were on a lonely stretch of the highway with farms and forest on either side of the road. "We're on the last leg of the journey," said Mason.

"Nice. So we'll be in Beaver Run soon. It's been a long trip. You know, you're such a good driver. I rarely sleep in a car, but I slept like a baby."

That explains it, thought Mason. *She was asleep.*

Priyanka opened the chocolate box again and picked one. "Here, try this. Open up."

He opened his mouth, and she pushed it in. He started to chew. It was delicious. "Hmm, very good."

Suddenly a deer ran into the road, followed by two more. Mason's breath caught. He knew the drill. Slow down, don't swerve.

He stepped on the brake and gripped the steering wheel tighter.

The first two deer ran across. The third one suddenly changed its mind and decided to run back. Then stopped dead center in front of the car. *Don't swerve! Don't swerve!*

Priyanka screamed.

He didn't swerve. Neither did the car stop. There was a sickening thud, the screech of tires, and Mason felt like his heart dropped into his stomach. The car skidded, then bounced as they climbed over something, probably the deer, and finally came to a stop at the shoulder of the road.

Mason looked in the rearview mirror. Cars on the road had slowed down. A tangled mess with limbs sticking in different directions lay in the road with a wet trail leading back to the car.

His hand shook. His head throbbed. His heartbeat seemed to have relocated to his head. Mason took a deep breath and said, "Are you okay?"

"Oh God...is...is it dead?"

Mason looked at the rearview mirror again. "I think so. Yes. It is dead. But are you okay?"

"I think so," said Priyanka, then turned to look at him. Her eyes widened. "Your head. You're hurt."

Mason felt throbbing in his head. He touched his forehead, and it felt sticky. Then he felt pain. "What the—?" Then he noticed the visor was halfway down. He must have hit his head on it during impact.

"Here." With shaky hands, Priyanka passed him a paper napkin from their last stop.

Mason turned the car off and got out. The smell of rubber, hot engine oil, and fresh meat like a butcher's stall filled the air. Orange liquid dripped out of the car, forming a small pool on the ground. Cars slowed down as they passed.

"Are you okay sir?" said a voice behind Mason.

He whirled around to see a middle-aged man. His fully loaded sedan was parked not too far behind him. Mason hadn't seen him pull over.

"Yes...the deer came from nowhere."

"Yeah, they're everywhere. Once it's fuck season for them, they lose their minds. Excuse my French. I've hit a few myself. Have you called 911?"

Mason tapped his pocket. "No, my phone is in the car." He turned to go back.

"I'll call them," said the guy. "It's straightforward. They'll take a report. You'll probably need a rental car too, and have that head looked at."

"Thank you," said Mason. He went to the passenger side of the pathfinder. Priyanka had her hands wrapped around her. The chocolate tray was empty, the contents scattered all over the floor. "Are you sure you're okay?"

She nodded and looked at him with wet, dull eyes. "Yeah, but you're the one bleeding." Her voice was shaky.

Mason stopped. She'd been crying. "It's just a small gash from the sun visor." He cupped her face between his palm and kissed her on the forehead.

The EMT that came with the ambulance cleaned his wound. It was just a scratch. By the time they finished with the police, had the car towed away, and dealt with the rental company, it was five in the evening. The drive back had been mostly quiet. Dr. Patel had called asking what was keeping them. Not to panic him, they'd agreed to tell him they had car trouble and had to switch cars with the rental agency. They should be in Beaver Run in about an hour.

"I'll need to make one stop before I drop you off," said Mason as he tapped his phone screen and put in a new address. Ten minutes later, he turned into a parking lot.

"Cupid Cabana?" said Priyanka when he pulled into the parking lot.

"I won't stay long. You can come in and use the bathroom. Or I can get you something?"

She shook her head. "No, I just want to go home."

Mason nodded and dashed into the building. Ten minutes later, he was back in the car. "I hope I didn't take too long."

Priyanka raised her chin. "No that's fine." She let out a humorless laugh. "Cupid Cabana. You're following up with your original plan."

Mason exhaled. "I might as well. Like you said, there were a lot of contingencies we didn't take into account. Then there's the horoscope compatibility issue."

"So you laid it all out to Cupid?" said Priyanka.

"I was lucky once with when I rubbed John Harvard's shoe. Who knows?" He started the car. "Sorry for the wait. There was a bit of a line."

"You know I can take an Uber from here."

"Why? It's not necessary." He pulled out of the space, drove out of the parking lot, and got back on the road. "My job is to get you home, not Uber you home."

The rest of the drive to Beaver Run was done in silence. No talking between them, just love songs from the radio in the background. As they approached the destination according to the GPS, Mason felt his heart beating faster. He started to feel hot. This was it.

He turned on the inside light, reached into his pocket, and pulled out his wallet. He fished out a business card. "I would have taken your number but…until you get a new phone. This is my business card. We can keep in touch…or send me a text or email when you get a new number."

She looked at him, sniffed, and wiped her nose. "Okay." She took the card and put it in her pocket.

The GPS alerted Mason when they arrived at their destination, and Mason drove in. "Nice house." It was a mansion with a three-car garage and manicured lawn with lights pointing in different directions showing the beauty of the grounds and the house.

The front door opened, and a man about fifty and a middle-aged woman rushed out. The woman descended the stairs fast, arms open, a stricken, worried look on her face.

"Priyanka! Priyanka!" said the woman, coming toward the car as Priyanka got out. "My daughter! My daughter!" She swept her into a huge embrace.

The man approached. "Pri! Pri." He joined in the group hug.

Mason got out of the car and took a few steps toward the front of the vehicle. He could see the resemblance. Priyanka took after her mother. Seeing the family reunited and happy left a warm fuzzy feeling in his heart.

"Mason!" said Dr. Patel, untangling himself from his wife, who was now speaking to Priyanka in accented English. He walked toward Mason.

"Dr. Patel." Mason extended his hand.

"Sanjay, Sanjay," said Dr. Patel and gave Mason a bro hug.

"I'm sorry…Sanjay."

Dr. Patel slapped him on the back. "Thank you for bringing my princess back home."

9

MASON

IT WAS BITTERSWEET FOR MASON THAT THE JOURNEY WAS
over and Priyanka safely back home. He was too tired, but he
still needed to drive another forty minutes or so to get home.
It occurred to him that since he was in Beaver Run, he might
drop in and see Stone. He called ahead. Stone was at a place
called the Beaver Tail Bar and asked him to come over.
Mason didn't need the rowdiness of a bar right now and
wanted to pass. But Stone assured him it was more of a
restaurant than a bar.

Stone was right. The smell of food greeted him once he
opened the door. The dining room was laid out as in any other
restaurant. Families with children sat at some of the tables
enjoying dinner. He spotted Stone in the bar.

"My brother from another mother!" said Stone, giving
him a bro hug. "You look like shit. Did someone die on you?"

Mason chuckled. "Hi, bro, good to see you too. Just came
back from Georgia. It was one hell of a road trip."

"Oh, yes. The job with Dr. Patel's daughter." His eyes narrowed. "I'm guessing everything went well since you're here."

Mason nodded. "Long story, but it went well."

"I love long stories, but before you start, this is my boss, Trevor Leigh." He pointed at the young man sitting next to him. "Trevor, Mason. Mason, Trevor."

They both pointed at each other and went, "Oh!"

"See, see?" said Stone. "You've both already heard about each other."

"Nice to finally meet you," said Trevor. "I've heard a lot of good things about you. And don't listen to him. I'm not his boss. We're both deputies, just that he's a new implant to Beaver Run."

"Great to finally meet you too," said Mason. "Heard a lot of good things. Read about you in the papers too. Glad everything worked out fine."

Trevor clapped his hands together. "Luck was on our side. What's your poison of choice? Beer? Whiskey?"

Mason laughed. "Beer is fine."

Trevor raised his hand. "Sandra, we need some service here."

"Coming," said a pretty blonde at the other end of the bar.

Stone shifted to the next stool. "Sit right here in the middle, Mason." He lowered his voice. "So did you go to Cupid Cabana?"

"Yes, about an hour ago. Stopped there first before dropping off Priyanka."

"I thought you left with the first flight yesterday morning," said Stone.

"Yes, but we drove back. Thirteen hours, no joke."

"What do you want, Trevor?" asked the blonde coming to a halt in front of them.

"This is Stone's buddy from college, Mason. My sister Sandra. She owns the bar-"

"Co-owner," said Sandra and smiled. "Nice to meet you, Mason. What can I get for you?"

Mason locked eyes with her. He felt a tingling at the base of his neck. "Any draft beer is fine."

Her eyes lingered. "Okay." She turned, got a clean glass, and poured him a beer from the tap. "Enjoy." She walked away.

"So you flew into Atlanta and then drove back?" Stone shrugged. "I know you're scared of flying, but you already overcame that by flying in."

"The plane skidded off the runway after we landed."

"What! I would pee my pants too," said Trevor.

Mason told them everything from the plane crash experience to hitting a deer on I-95 over a few more mugs of beer and some chicken wings. He excluded every detail about Priyanka.

"What about Dr. Patel's daughter?" asked Stone.

Mason's heart missed a beat. "What about her?"

"The way you avoided mentioning her, it sounds like she just went into the backseat and slept all the way from Georgia to New Jersey."

Mason cocked his head. "Something like that."

They all laughed.

Mason yawned. "I have to head out. I'm beat, guys."

"No, you're not," said Stone. "We are not driving either." He pulled out his phone and tapped on the screen. "I practically live at Adela's farm now. So I use Airbnb to lease out my home sometimes until Adela and I have more concrete plans on what to do with it. I know I have someone coming soon. Let me check."

"So if it's free, Sandra can drop him off there since it's on her way," said Trevor.

Mason didn't like the direction the night was going. Maybe he should just drive back to Elkwood.

Stone stared at his screen. "Yes, I have a Lucas Martin coming in the next few weeks, so it's free now."

"Wait a minute," said Trevor. "Did you say Lucas Martin?"

"Yeah, do you know him?"

"Yes, if it's the same Lucas. He and Sandra were sweet on each other way back. Then he moved."

"Okay, at least he's not at the house yet, so Sandra can drop him," said Stone.

"How are you guys getting home?"

"Sarah's coming to get me. We have a candlelit dinner to go to," said Trevor.

Stone smiled. "Sweet Adela is coming for me. We're having dinner in the loft in the barn. Sandra—Trevor is talking to Sandra now. I hope she'll be able to drop you off at my place. It's on her way."

Mason wondered if he'd made a mistake stopping to see Stone. He and Sandra had made eye contact. Now they were being left alone. That wasn't such a great idea in his book.

"Where's the victim I'm dropping off?" said a familiar voice behind them.

Mason turned. It was Sandra. She'd let her hair down and removed her apron. She had a lot of hair, and her legs seemed to go on forever into a mini skirt.

"He's right here," said Trevor. "It was a pleasure meeting you. Hope to see more of you."

"Same here," said Mason.

Stone slapped him on the back. "I'll call you. The key is under the dry grass in the gargoyle shaped flowerpot. You can't miss it. If there's anything you can't find, just give me a call."

"I'm ready when you are," said Sandra.

"Ready."

Sandra drove an F-150. Mason had expected a sedan, but a truck made sense, especially considering the business.

"Which one is your car?" asked Sandra as she pulled out of the parking lot. "I have to let the guy closing know so they don't think it was abandoned and call a tow truck."

"Oh, it's the Pathfinder over there." He pointed at it.

She pulled out her phone and spoke into it. She hung it on a magnet on her dash when she was done. "Thank God for speech to text. It's a lot easier to send a text without taking your eyes off the road."

"You're right. I always forget to use it."

"Stone's house is not far away. We should be there within minutes. So you and Sam go back a long way."

Mason nodded. "Yes. High school, then college."

"That's a solid friendship right there. Good for you guys. Is this your first time in Beaver Run?"

"Yes. Just drove in from Georgia—"

"That's an ass-numbing trip. I did it once."

"I agree. I should have just gone straight home to Elkwood. But I thought since I was already in town, I might as well see Stone. Glad I did. It's amazing the experience he and your brother had."

Sandra nodded. "There are bad people in this world."

They drove in silence for a few more minutes listening to music. She liked country music.

The click click click of the indicator broke the monotony before Sandra pulled into the driveway of a ranch.

"Here we are. I told you it wasn't far."

"Thanks so much. I'm just going to get in there and pass out."

Sandra smiled. "You look tired. Did he give you the key?"

"No, he mentioned something about the statue of a devil or…"

Sandra laughed. "I better come and help you before you spend the night out here looking for a devil statue long after I'm gone. It's a gargoyle flowerpot."

Mason watched as she got out of the car and flashed a lot of thigh as she stepped out. He swallowed, wishing she'd just dropped him off and left.

10

PRIYANKA

PRIYANKA CHECKED IF THE WATERCOLOR PAINTING WAS DRY.
She looked at it one more time and smiled. She picked up the
can of fixative and sprayed it over the dry artwork. First hori-
zontal, then vertical. Once ready, she had a sleeve for it.

Behind the business card Mason had given her was an
address in Elkwood, New Jersey. She'd gone online, typed in
Mason Sutton and Elkwood, and one of the returns was the
same address. Google map showed it to be a residential area.
It could only be his home. She couldn't keep away anymore.

Priyanka's job as an artist was simple—just stay home
and paint. In her third year of college, she'd gotten a gig to
paint an oil realism portrait on canvas of an internet startup's
founding members. By the time she graduated, that startup
had become a multi-billion-dollar company.

The founders were media-shy and reclusive. The only
option was to use her portrait of them. Her painting was
featured on magazine covers and on social media almost

every time the founders were mentioned, giving her wide exposure.

It opened the flood gate of six-figure commissions, and she could literally work from anywhere. Since she wasn't 'chasing' work and the family house had ample space, it seemed logical to paint at home. Then her father had gotten his dream job in New Jersey, and they moved.

The first few days after she got back from Georgia, her mother had pampered her. She didn't bother her about anything related to getting married or looking at matrimonial ads.

But Priyanka had seen her perusing a physical copy of the Indian Guardian she'd gotten from an Indian shop in Morris County. Pencil in hand, she would circle ads for further investigation. It was only a matter of time before she started pestering her again.

It'd been six days since Mason had dropped her off. She'd replaced her phone the very next day, sure she would call him. Priyanka would bring up his business card, hold it in one hand and her new phone in the other, trying to gather enough courage to make the call. There was no doubt she was in love with him, but there were obstacles she had no control over. That was one side of it. Then there was him. Did he feel the same?

She put the package in the car, told her mother she was going to the mall, and took off. She didn't like telling her mother lies, but telling her the truth wouldn't win her any brownie points.

As she drove her BMW to Elkwood, she was tempted to take an exit ramp and return to Beaver Run many a time. What if he wasn't home? Or he had company? Maybe he'd already forgotten her and moved on. Okay, if it came to that, then she would just drop off the package.

Why couldn't her mother be as cool as her dad, she wondered.

The address was a one-story building in a beautiful cul-de-sac. She wasn't sure it was the right place, but there was something familiar about it. As she walked toward the door, she realized it was the Pathfinder in the driveway. It was the same model as the one they'd driven from Atlanta.

Priyanka remembered him insisting that they got a Pathfinder as a replacement after they hit the deer. Familiarity. He'd rented a car he was familiar with. Confident, she rang the bell.

As she waited, she looked at what she was wearing. A brown ribbed sweater over a knee-length black leather skirt and ankle-length suede boots. Was she overdressed? She raised her head to the sound of the door being unlocked.

The door swung open. A frowning Mason wearing a black T-shirt over basketball shorts with a five-day stubble stared down at her. Then his eyes widened, and a big smile appeared on his face.

"Pri! Pri!" He opened the door wider. "Oh my God, what are you doing here? Did your dad send you? He could have just called or sent me a text."

Just seeing him set off a fluttery feeling in her stomach. She shook her head. "I couldn't keep away any longer. I came to see you."

He scooped her into his arms and spun her around.

Priyanka yelped. She laughed as she held his shoulder for support. A warm feeling started from her chest and spread all over her body. "Put me down, put me down," she said and giggled. "People might see."

He didn't put her down but stopped spinning her. "I'll only put you down if you kiss me."

68

Heat rushed to her cheeks. "Oh God." She brushed her hair back, leaned forward, and kissed him on the cheeks.

Mason shook his head. "No."

She laughed and threw her head back. She leaned forward to kiss his cheeks again, and he faked her out and took her lips.

Oh, she felt like she was home. Mason smelled of his cologne, masculine, spicy, and with a dash of citrus. His lips were warm and soft against hers. The world seemed to stop and stand still, peaceful, punctuated with the rapid drumming of her heart against her rib cage.

He pulled back and looked into her eyes. "I love you, Priyanka Patel. I don't know what I'll do without you. You've taken over my dreams. You make me complete. You said to stay away, and—"

Her vision got cloudy. "I…I love you too, Mason. I couldn't stay away."

He carried her into the house and pulled the door shut.

11

PRIYANKA

"THIS IS THE LIVING ROOM," SAID MASON. HE WALKED A FEW more steps. "This is the kitchen. The half bath is down that way." He went up the stairs.

Priyanka cycled her legs and laughed. "You know I can walk." His hard cock pressing against her body drove her crazy. She knew her pussy was getting flooded, her panties drenched.

"Yep, I'll put you down soon. The guest room is that way, and this is the bathroom." Mason nudged the door open with his leg. "And this is the master bedroom." He laid her down on the king-sized bed.

Priyanka's body was on fire. She wanted to touch him, feel his hard body against hers. She sat up on the bed, supporting herself on her elbows, looking at him.

"God, I missed you. I just want to spread you out on the bed and devour you. Tell me what you want, Pri, and I'll give it to you."

A shudder shot through her. "I want you inside me. All of you." Her voice was a whimper.

He shook his head. "Since the first time I set eyes on you, I wanted to devour you. Virginia was a preamble, and I didn't get to taste you." He stroked her leg as he spoke.

Priyanka shivered, and goosebumps sprouted all over her skin.

"I'm not just going to fuck you. I'll take my time, bury my face between those long sexy legs of yours. I'm not going to skip over that part."

Priyanka shut her eyes and let out a shaky breath. Yes, she wanted that. The softness of his tongue on her pussy lips. Most of all, she wanted the loss of control that came with that kind of touch. "Yes, I'd like that."

He hovered over her and took her lips. He pulled back, nibbled her lips, and brushed his lips against her neck, her chest, stomach, and her crotch through her skirt.

Her pulse raced. The feathery touch felt so good.

Mason continued down to her thighs, caressing her all the way to her ankle. He took off her boot and massaged her foot.

"Oh, that feels good," Priyanka moaned. She'd been working the gas and brake pedals with that foot for the past hour. He kneaded it, firing off jolts of electric charges to her pussy. "Yes."

Mason kissed her toes, licked his way to her thighs, his fingers massaging and kneading her muscles. "Your legs are spectacular," he said with a groan.

He did the same with the other leg. He ran his hand under her skirt. He squeezed her butt, and as his hands exited, he peeled off her soaked panties. Next to come off was her skirt, leaving her naked from the waist down.

Her breath hitched. She wanted Mason to touch her, to feel the flood he'd unleashed between her legs.

His head hovered over her crotch, feasting his eyes as if deciding where to take the first bite from. He brushed her public hair with the stubble on his chin as he slid his hands under her sweater and under her bra. He grabbed a handful of her breast, rolled her nipple in his finger, and had her writhing on the bed.

Priyanka spread her legs wider. The expectation of what he would do next drove her insane. She grabbed his hair and tried to direct his head to where she wanted it to be, but he had other plans.

He lowered his head and went to work. A rumbling sound from his throat showed he enjoyed what he was doing. Mason nibbled on her pussy lips, lapping up the juices dripping out of her core.

"Oh God, Jesus." She squeezed his head between her thighs. His mouth on her felt so good. Priyanka felt like her head was going to explode. She was already on the mountain edge. A gust of wind would tip her over. She moaned. "Mason, eat it."

"Why?"

She gasped. "Why…why? I want to come…make me come."

"Say please."

She wanted to come so badly. She reached for her pussy to do the job herself.

Mason slapped her hand away and hovered, poised like a dog waiting to hear the word fetch.

She twisted and pushed her hips up. The stubbornness in her wouldn't let her say the word, but her body demanded that. "Please," she moaned, drawing out the word. "Make me come."

Like a dog tossed a bone, Mason fastened his lips on her core. He licked, nibbled, and pulled as if it would be taken away from him before he had his fill.

Priyanka's breath hitched. A shudder tore through her, and her orgasm ripped through her like a cannon shot.

Mason pulled his T-shirt off and removed his shorts. He'd been commando underneath them. His cock, now set free, nodded with every beat of his heart. He leaned forward and kissed her lips long and hard.

Priyanka could taste the saltiness of her juices on his lips. She only drew back when she was close to breathless, her heart pounding so hard as if it would tumble out of her chest. "You are just wonderful. I love-"

They both gasped when his cock slid into her. She was ready to be taken up that hill again.

Mason was relentless. His cock went in and out, his speed increasing as his groans got louder and louder. He found the right angle for maximum pleasure and drove into her wet pussy again and again, chasing his orgasm.

Her nails dug into his back. She was gasping as much as he was, thrusting her hips upward to meet him.

And when he came, screaming her name, he pulled her along with him.

By the time Priyanka got home that night, her body was exhausted and satisfied, but her heart ached. Their love was like that of Romeo and Juliet. She was an adult, and her parents really didn't have dominion over her. But it would be good to have their blessing.

She wondered what to do. She'd given Mason the Taj Mahal painting she drew for him, and he'd remembered their conversation.

"A symbol of your love for me," he'd said. "I've never seen a better painting. I'll never stop loving you as long as I draw breath."

Priyanka parked her car in the garage and pushed the

button to lower the garage door. She entered through the kitchen door and saw her mom coming toward her, excited.

"I heard you drive in. I've been waiting." She waved a copy of the Indian Guardian in her hand. "Oh, my daughter. Finally, we have a match."

12

MASON

MASON HAD BEEN SURPRISED BUT OVERJOYED TO SEE Priyanka when she came to his house. As far as he was concerned, their connection was a match made in heaven. They were on the same page, destined to be together. Only one obstacle was in their way, and Mason did not know how to tackle that.

He'd gotten an email from the ads broker in India that his ad was popular, and a few responses wanted to meet right away. But only one had a compatible horoscope. Mason replied that he would like to meet with the compatible horoscope. He held his breath as he waited for the email with the address and date of where to meet. When it came, the address was in Beaver Run, New Jersey.

The main problem he had was how to convince her parents that they were right for each other. His own parents would go along with him. They'd always trusted him with making his own decisions, which sometimes was scary. He imagined what his father would say, 'Son, do you love her? Does she love you? If the answer is yes, then you will win the war. There will be challenges, battles along the way, but only the love you have for each other can sustain you to win the war in the long run.'

The appointment was for a Friday evening, and Mason decided to call on Dr. Patel on the same day with the bill for services rendered. How do they say it, kill two birds with one stone?

The insurance company absorbed the damage from the accident with the deer, so all he billed for was his time. He fired off an email with the invoice as an attachment to Dr. Patel.

When he arrived at Beaver Run, he remembered the last time he was there. He'd met Stone, Trevor, and Sandra. He was glad Sandra had offered to help him find the key. The flowerpot he had in mind wasn't what was there. He would have looked forever.

Sandra had left her bar early because she had a date. She wished Mason a good night's sleep and a safe trip tomorrow and left. He'd slept like a puppy.

Stone came in the morning early with Adela on their way to drop off eggs and gave him a ride back to the bar. They agreed to meet up again soon, and he picked up his car and went home.

"You've arrived."

Mason's GPS drew him out of his reverie. He drove up to Patel's mansion and parked. He was sweating bullets despite having the window down in the chilly February night.

Mason walked up the flight of stairs hoping that Priyanka would come to the door. But he hadn't told her of his plan, so she wasn't expecting him. His heart beating like a tabla drum, he rang the bell.

"Ding dong." Sounded somewhere inside the house.

Mason heard footsteps approach the elegant stained frosted glass door. Anybody but Mrs. Patel could come to the door, and he would be fine.

When the door swung open, it was his friend Sanjay there. Mason was overtaken with giddiness and an unexpected release of tension. "Good to see you, sir!"

"Mason! This is a pleasant surprise." Dr. Patel smiled and looked him over. "Are you going somewhere fancy? You're all dressed up."

"Good evening, Sanjay." Mason hesitated. "No...well yes." His eyebrows narrowed. "I...I sent you a text. I was in the neighborhood—Sorry, is this a bad time?"

"Text? No, not at all. Come in, come in. Are you sure?"

"Yes, I sent the invoice earlier by email. Since I was in the neighborhood, I thought I'd drop in." Mason stepped into the well-lit foyer with a high ceiling from which dangled a chandelier the size of an SUV. "Wow, that's the biggest chandelier I've ever seen. Nice décor."

Two staircases on opposite ends of the wall led upstairs. A half table with ornate carvings was pushed against the wall under a large gold-framed mirror. An antique-looking love seat was placed in a corner.

"Thank you. My wife loves to decorate." Dr. Patel slapped his hand against his forehead. "Sorry, I put my phone in the study so I wouldn't be distracted. I've been scurrying around like a squirrel following orders. My wife has a guest coming and is overly excited."

Mason swallowed. His heart dropped into this stomach like a boulder. There was no turning back; he was here already. He prayed it would end well.

His stomach growled. "It does smell great in here."

"Yes." Dr. Patel looked away, avoiding eye contact with Mason.

An uneasy awkward silence passed between them. Under normal circumstances at this point, Dr. Patel should have asked him to stay for dinner to fill the void. And offer to add an extra chair to the table.

Dr. Patel exhaled. "Why don't you come into my study? There'll be less distraction there." He led the way, and Mason followed.

His study was as exquisitely furnished as the foyer and glimpses of the living room Mason had seen. Once Dr. Patel shut the door behind him, it kept away the sounds from the rest of the house.

A huge ornate desk sat in the middle of the room with a leather executive swivel chair on one side and two similar chairs on the other side. An Apple iMac was centered on the table with a few medical magazines around it. Two book-shelves filled with books were flush against one wall.

Dr. Patel pointed at one of the two leather seats. "Have a seat." He walked around to the opposite side and sat down. He opened a drawer and pulled out his phone.

Mason wanted to say something, but he couldn't think of the right thing. But this was an opportunity to sell himself to the doctor.

"I'm so happy my wife finally found a horoscope match," said Dr. Patel and slid his finger across his phone screen. He broke out in a smile.

"Horoscope match?"

"Yes, there's this matching game she likes to play. They call it Matrimonial Ads. Sometimes good things come out of it, so you have to keep on trying."

Mason swallowed. He was heating up again and pulled at the collar of his shirt. This was his chance to own up.

"Ah, I see the invoice. Sutton securities." He glanced up and looked at Mason.

Mason raised his eyebrows.

"And you're the CEO? Wait a minute. The name sounds familiar." Dr. Patel snapped his fingers. "I'm on a hospital committee that awarded a million-dollar contract to Sutton Securities not too long ago for some cutting-edge security equipment and service." He rubbed his chin, blinking rapidly. "You didn't need to go to Atlanta. You could have sent somebody to pick up Pri."

"Well, Sam Stone told me personally about the job last September. So this was a follow-up since I was supposed to handle it then." Mason laughed nervously. "Remember, it was supposed to be an easy assignment. It just got complicated."

Dr. Patel cocked his head, eyebrows narrowed. He looked at his phone, then at Mason. He got up, walked to the bookshelf, and picked up a newspaper. "How old are you?"

"Twenty-eight."

"How tall are you? Six two?"

Sweat poured down Mason's face. "Yes."

"And you graduated from MIT!" Dr. Patel tossed the paper down and collapsed into his chair. He cradled his head in his hands. "You put a matrimonial ad in an Indian newspaper?"

There was a brief silence. "Yes, sir."

Dr. Patel's head shot up. "Pri helped you, didn't she? Oh God, my wife will…"

Mason sat and watched, not sure what to do.

Dr. Patel groaned and shook his head. "I should have seen that. I was so happy to have her back. She told me about trying to run away from you by climbing down from her balcony. Because she thought you were one of the people that stole her phone." Dr. Patel smiled. "Then feeding you hot peppers, and you asked her if Indians went on special training to learn how to eat hot and spicy food. Then the accident—I thought the whole thing was just an adventure for her. I could tell she has a soft spot for you." He rubbed his hands together, then held them under his chin as if in prayer. "Mason, do you love my daughter?"

Mason sat up and looked him straight in the eye. "Dr. Patel, with all my heart."

He nodded. "What about your parents? This is a journey—you're Caucasian, she's Indian. It could be…"

"I know, sir. My family will fall in line. I know our love will see us through. I'd love to marry Priyanka."

Dr. Patel raked his fingers through his hair and sighed. "Pri's happiness is my greatest concern. Your horoscopes are compatible, you're well settled…if she says it's you, then you have my blessing."

Mason couldn't believe his ears. He felt like jumping into the air and giving Dr. Patel a hug.

Dr. Patel chuckled. "Maybe it's my turn to run away like Pri. My wife isn't going to find this funny."

Mason felt like a boulder had been lifted off his shoulders. "Thank you, sir, thank you."

Dr. Patel got up, shaking his head. "No, no, don't thank me yet. Like I said, you have my blessing. I'm now going to tell my wife that the horoscope compatibility she's been raving about is with you."

"Do…do you have to tell her? Isn't your blessing alone good enough?"

Dr. Patel shook his head sadly. "I'm only the head of household. Depending on how I deliver this bad news there might be a lot of eating out in my future."

Mason got up, wishing there was a way he could convince him not to leave the room.

Dr. Patel stopped at the door and pointed. "That double patio door leads into the garden. I just thought I'd share that information with you." He shrugged. "Just in case…"

Moments later, Mason heard a lot of screaming and rapid-fire Hindi. It was quickly followed by the sound of plates smashing and more screaming. Within seconds, Mason found himself holding the handle to the patio door.

13

PRIYANKA (ONE WEEK Later)

PRIYANKA STOOD IN THE FOYER OF THEIR HOME, WAITING FOR Mason to get to the door. It was February the 27th. She'd been checking the calendar on her phone by the hour to remind herself that February was twenty-eight days. It could be twenty-nine, but not thirty or thirty-one like the other months. Otherwise, their best-laid plans would come to nothing.

She looked around the space, then up at the massive chandelier with its brand-new light bulbs and crystals. The guys that changed it did an amazing job. No one would be able to tell it was a completely new chandelier unless they had been here when it happened. Her mind drifted to that night.

Priyanka was upset her mother had set up another date so soon. She'd agreed to come down for dinner, but late. However, the sound of breaking glass and shouts made her come down sooner rather than later, thinking an earthquake or something like that was happening.

The whole floor was covered in pieces of broken crystals and light bulbs. She was lucky she had shoes on.

"What happened?"

Father explained that her mother had lost it after learning that Mason was the person whose horoscope was compatible with hers and was here for the dinner date. She'd started smashing dinner plates. And when she exhausted them, she'd grabbed a stool to reach a higher cupboard for more dishes.

Father tried to stop her, and as they struggled for the stool, it catapulted into the chandelier.

Priyanka was dumbfounded by the destruction. One of these days, somebody would be directly or indirectly hurt by this madness. Then she realized what her father said and squealed with delight. What? Their horoscope was compatible, and Mason had come to meet her parents.

Her mother had directed her anger at her once she noticed she was there.

"You! What is wrong with you?" said her mother, wagging an accusatory finger. "Every nice man we find for you is not good enough. We ask you to study a worthy course —medicine, engineering, pharmacy, law, but no. We give you everything you want, and how do you pay us back? You—"

Father cleared his throat. He looked at his wife with pleading eyes. "*Meree nanhee chidiya*, my little bird…"

Mother turned and glared at him. He backed away, and she refocused on Priyanka. "You chose to go to Boston University when you could have gone to Harvard. Fine. You got a degree in drawing and painting"—she waved her hand in the air as if painting with a brush—"when you had the grades to study law. Fine. But one thing I ask of you is to marry an Indian boy. That is the only thing we ask of you."

Something snapped inside Priyanka. She'd never stood up to her mother. Her chest heaved like she'd just finished a fifty-meter dash. Adrenaline loosened her lips as she faced her mother.

Her mother didn't back away. Her eyes shot daggers at her daughter.

Priyanka's nose flared. "Listen to yourself. Everything you've said is we, we, we. What about me? What about what I want? It's my life at the end of the day. I have tried to please you all my life, but it's never enough. I was born here in America. What I know is the way of life here. I don't have anything against any Indian boy or American boy or my Indian heritage. This—"

"You don't listen to what you're told." Mother turned to her husband. "Sanjay, you have to say something."

Priyanka faced her dad. "Father, why did you leave India and move to America?"

"I came for a better life. More opportunities—"

"But you could have gone back after your education. Maybe if I'd been born in India and grown up there, I would understand things better." Priyanka let out a shaky breath. "It's about who you connect with, no matter the package it comes in. You wanted me to study medicine, apply to Harvard, and marry the man of your dreams. I don't like medicine. I love to draw and paint—and I'm good at it. I earn six figures for each piece. Why would I do what I don't enjoy and make myself unhappy? When tough times come, it's almost impossible to dig in and hang in there when you don't like what you're doing in the first place. I didn't apply to an Ivy League school because it wasn't where I wanted to be. The boy of your dreams is not the man of my own dreams. We—"

"Okay, time out!" said Father. He made the time out signal frantically.

Tears rolled down Priyanka's cheeks. "The ad was my

idea, Mother. Since you wanted to find someone for me to marry, I decided to use it to my advantage. To create a big fat matrimonial ad that would meet your requirements and mine. But guess what, we didn't even have to lie in the ad. Everything we put in it was true. And yet, when our horoscope was compatible—something we couldn't predict—you still didn't want it. I can't marry someone you find for me."

Mother sighed and folded her hands over her chest. "And why not?"

"I'm in love with Mason. I was stuck with him in a car for almost twenty-four hours, and somehow, we connected. How did I meet Mason? Because I ran away from home to avoid the pressure of meeting someone I didn't want. I got mugged, got in an accident. It could have been worse. Then what? Do I have to die—?"

"Okay, that's enough," said Father. "Don't talk to your mother like that."

Mother stood still like something made from wood, her eyes as wide as golf balls.

Priyanka sobbed and clasped her hand over her mouth. "I'm so sorry for my outburst…so sorry…please forgive me." She ran back upstairs, crunching glass under the sole of her shoes.

Her father yelled, "Pri, be careful! The glass…"

She went to her room and cried. Later her father came in, and she sobbed on his shoulder.

"It's okay, my little princess. I understand your position. Your mother and I only want what's best for you."

The sound of someone at the door brought her out of her reminiscing. She opened the door, and there was Mason dressed casually in khaki pants, a white shirt, and a blazer.

He leaned back and looked her over. His lips parted with

lust and love in his eyes. "Hi. You are breathtaking." He kissed her cheek.

Heat rushed through her. "Thank you, but save your schmoozing for the right people. They're already waiting, come on." Mason followed her to the dining room.

"Father, Mother...my boyfriend, Mason Sutton."

"Dr. Patel, Mrs. Patel, good evening."

"Hi, Mason," said Dr. Patel. "Sit, sit." He smiled at Mason.

"Hello, Mason," said Priyanka's mom. "Good to see you again. The last time you left in a hurry through—"

"Ummm...Let's not dwell in the past," said Dr. Patel quickly. "Mason! I hope you like Indian food. My wife took the liberty of preparing the food without the heat for tonight's dinner."

"That's very generous of her. Thank you," said Mason and nodded toward Mrs. Patel. "Yes, I do like Indian food, and the house smells delicious." He glanced at Priyanka sitting beside him and smiled. "But before we start, there's something I'd like to say."

Pri's heart thumped in her chest like galloping horses. *Oh God, what's he going to say? Things have been perfect so far.* Her eyes darted to her parents then back to Mason.

Mason stood and pushed his chair back. He faced Priyanka's parents. "Thank you so much for inviting me to dinner again at your home. I want to apologize for the matrimonial ad that caused a lot of confusion earlier. I know our backgrounds are different, but I'm willing to learn. I know the journey ahead will have its challenges, but our love for each other will be our lighthouse in the storm." He turned and looked at Priyanka. "I would walk through fire for you, Pri."

Eyes brimming with tears, Priyanka nodded. Her lips quivered, trying to decide whether to laugh or cry.

Mason reached into his pocket, brought out a small box, and dropped to one knee. He opened it to show a ring.

Priyanka gasped. Her hands flew to her mouth.

"Priyanka Patel. I love you so much, with all my heart. Will you marry me?"

Her jaw dropped. She looked at her parents, then back at Mason. "Yes! Yes!" She stared at the ring, not believing her eyes as he slid it onto her finger.

Dr. Patel beamed. "Wow, this calls for a toast." He shot up from his chair, knocking it over, and rushed to the buffet and hutch. He opened a cupboard and retrieved a bottle of champagne.

Priyanka looked at her mother and saw tears in her eyes. She went and hugged her.

Her mother squeezed her tight. "I'm happy for you. You found love. I was only trying to do things the way I under-stand," she said in a whisper. "But one size doesn't fit all. Please forgive me, and I'm very, very proud of you."

Priyanka hugged her tighter. "Thank you, Mother. It means so much to me."

"Okay, okay, grab your flutes," said Dr. Patel. Then he muttered to himself, "Before the moment passes. Next thing you two will start fighting." He raised his glass. "To Mason and Priyanka. May all you wish for yourselves come through. May your future be blessed."

They all clicked glasses and took a sip.

"This is chicken tikka masala, butter naan, and cumin rice," said Mrs. Patel and pointed at the dishes.

Mason loaded his plate. "Nice." He tore off a butter naan and started to chew. Then he shoveled some rice and tikka masala into his mouth. "Delicious!"

"I agree," said Dr. Patel. "That's why I agreed to marry her."

Priyanka smiled and watched Mason eat. Suddenly, Mason was chewing and blowing at the same time.

"Water. Gosh…it's hot, spicy. I…"

Dr. Patel put down his fork, folded his hand across his chest, and stared at his wife. He said in a low voice, "My little bird…"

Mrs. Patel feigned innocence. "You heard the boy. He said he'd walk through fire for Pri."

EPILOGUE

PRIYANKA (ONE WEEK Later)

PRIYANKA STOOD IN FRONT OF THE EASEL WITH A PENCIL AND ran it over the white sketch paper. With her engagement, her mother now had peace of mind. She focused on her work and had some free time to pursue pet projects of her own.

She drew with long, strong, confident strokes. Priyanka stopped, took a step back, and examined her work. "So what do you think made our horoscope compatible? Cupid or the power of love?"

"Good question. Well, since love is involved and Cupid is the guy in charge of that, I'll say love."

She looked at him, then lowered her eyes. "Again?" said Priyanka in mock exaggeration. "Mason, another erection!"

Mason grinned sheepishly. "Sorry. You're the one that wanted to do a nude of me. I can't help myself. You're always on my mind."

"I'm flattered I'm always on your mind, but I'm here fully clothed and—"

"Not what I see in my mind. In my head, you're naked, spread out on my bed with lust in your eyes."

"You're lucky you're a computer engineer and don't have to make a living modeling for art students."

"What would happen when a model gets a hard-on while being sketched in class? I mean, has it ever happened?"

Priyanka tapped her pencil on her chin. "You know, I've never seen it happen before apart from here. If we were at my studio at home, this would never happen. The thought of my mom barging in at any time wouldn't even let you take off your clothes to be sketched. That would probably put your penis in retirement."

"Mm-hmm. That's why I said if you're going to sketch me naked, it's going to be at my home."

"But I've heard stories," said Priyanka. "It was a first-year class, and some of the girls had never seen a cock live before, and the poor guy got a hard-on."

"What happened?" asked Mason. "The girls surrounded him and got him off?"

"Ah, is that your fantasy? I'm not woman enough for you?"

"Pri, you're all the woman I would ever need and more."

She smiled. "Flattery. Anyway, if we had you as a model, you wouldn't last long. Once you get a hard-on that wouldn't go down, I'm sure you'd get kicked out, fired, and never be invited back for another modeling gig." She pointed her pencil at him. "Can you think of something terrible to make Mr. Happy go down so I can finish my sketch?"

"If you knew how many people I've murdered in my mind in the most gruesome way, I would be on the FBI's most-wanted list."

"If we had kids, I would be painting them, and they would be compliant." Priyanka sighed. "I guess I'll have to take care of it again." She took the pillow from the bed and walked toward him. She let it fall on the floor and dropped to her knees in front of him.

She could hear him breathing hard, and it made her excited, knowing the effect she had on him. His thick cock with engorged veins running on its surface stood pointing down at an incline from its sheer weight.

She looked up at him, and his eyes were pleading with her to take it in. She ran her wet tongue along his shaft, and his cock jumped as if he'd been touched with a live electric wire. Priyanka pulled back then giggled. "Excited, are we?"

"Baby, take it in your mouth," said Mason. His voice was thick with want.

She cupped his balls, weighed, and rolled them in her palm. She remembered when he had his lips over her pussy and wouldn't move until she begged for it. Revenge was always best served cold. "Say please."

Excitement seeped from the tip of his cock little by little, followed by groans that rumbled out from a place deep inside him. Those little moans traveled into her, shooting off sensations that caused her pussy to flood and soak her panties. Then she heard the magic word.

"Please, Pri. Take it in your mouth."

She opened her mouth and took in as much as she could and was immediately rewarded by the satisfying groan that escaped Mason's lips. She started to work on his cock. She used her hands, lips, and mouth, sliding, licking, and sucking. She started slowly, then picked up speed, bobbing her head forward and backward. Taking him in and out. Truth be told, she'd gotten enough practice in college as a compromise when her V card was on the table and she hadn't wanted to go all the way.

Mason let out a moan, and his legs started to shake. "Too much," he breathed.

Priyanka did not stop. She worked him faster, literally fucking him with her mouth.

Mason was on his tippy toes, gasping as she went faster and faster. "Baby, I can't—"

She took him to the edge and beyond, then felt a tap on her shoulder. It was a warning sign. All hell was going to break loose soon. Priyanka ignored the sign.

"Baby, I'm coming," said Mason, breathless. He let out a deep groan.

His whole body stiffened, and that was her cue. She wrapped her palms behind his butt and pulled him forward. She felt his eruption hit the back of her throat and held him in place until he was spent.

When he stopped shaking, she licked him clean and watched the look of amazement on his face, as if he wanted to ask where she'd learned how to do that. Then he changed his mind. Sometimes you don't want to know how sausages are made.

"Thank you," said Mason and curled up on his bed.

Priyanka joined him, and they held each other and dozed off. When she woke with a start an hour later, he was watching her.

"Hi," said Mason.

"Hi. I dozed off too."

"I'm memorizing every contour of your face," said Mason. "I love you."

Priyanka smiled. "I love you too."

"Is it okay if we moved our wedding forward? I don't think I can wait a whole year. I want us to start working on a family."

Priyanka sat up, her eyes shining. "Is it because of what I said earlier? Are you sure? That would make me very happy."

Mason nodded. "I'm sure. We found each other, and your happiness is my business."

They hugged and kissed.

The End

The series continues with Sandra and...
Click the image below to continue the series.

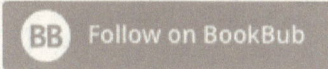

JOIN MY NEWSLETTER

Want to receive the latest information on my upcoming novels and receive a FREE book? Sign up for my free author newsletter by clicking on Brie Wilds Newsletter or visit www.briewilds.com

ABOUT THE AUTHOR

Brie Wilds is the author of My Big Fat Fake Matrimonial Ad, Book 3 of her Beaver Run Series. *Beaver Run* is a series of stand-alone, small-town, interconnected romance stories. Each book promises a complete, sweet, steamy, and happily ever after story.

Brie writes steamy, romance stories about men and women and their amazing and unique journey to finding happily ever after. Visit her website at www.briewilds.com for a free gift.

ALSO BY BRIE WILDS

The Stark Brother Series

Should I Say Yes

Never Been Loved

Love is Patient

The Stark Brothers Box Set

Cupid Cabana Series

Cupid Came Through

Maid for Him

Blame Cupid

Mountain Peak Series

The Neighbor Who Stole Christmas

Sleighing the Billionaire

Three Wise Men for Christmas

Beaver Run Series

Sarah's Secret

Kissed and Forgotten

My Big Fat Fake Matrimonial Ad

Beaver Run Reunion Series

Unbreak Her Heart

www.ingramcontent.com/pod-product-compliance
Lightning Source LLC
Chambersburg PA
CBHW011522100726
47899CB00010BD/3461